Catcher Interference (Tag & Skye Book 1)

A Columbia Gems Baseball Romance

MJ Compton

Comptonplations Publishing

CATCHER INTERFERENCE (TAG & SKYE BOOK 1)

The publisher does not have any control over and does not assume any responsibility for author or third-party websites or their content.

This book was previously published as MASKS OF OCTOBER

Original Release Date: October 25, 2016

CONTENTS

DEDICATION

To the Purples: Gayle Callen, Kris Fletcher, Carol Lombardo, and Christine Wenger, who are the best friends a writer could have. If not for their support, this novella would not have been written.

Acknowledgments

Micaela Compton, for her endless patience in answering restaurant/cooking questions.

Matthew Healy, brainstorming at the water cooler.

Elisa Konieczko, PhD, Full Professor of Biology, Gannon University (and fellow baseball fan) for help defining Tag's injury.

John Burt for insight into his wife Jessica's work as a Doctor of Physical Therapy.

TV Stevie for answering bizarre baseball questions.

October 20, Game 7 National League Championship Series

Tucker Alexander Gentry, known throughout the baseball universe as Tag, squatted behind home plate. His thigh muscles burned. He glared at the pitcher on the mound.

The entire season had come down to this moment. Game seven of the National League Championship Series. Top of the ninth inning. Two outs. The Columbia Gems were up by one, and Tag meant to keep the score that way. The tying run was on second base—some cocky wiseass New York had recently called up from Triple-A for the postseason. The go-ahead run was on first.

And Adam Chrestler, the Gems' closing pitcher, was shaking off Tag's signals. The oversize digital scoreboard played stupid cartoon graphics behind Chrestler's head. The ballpark was so silent Tag thought he heard the hot dog vendor on the third-base side of the stadium scouring his grill.

Tag thrust his hand between his splayed thighs and flashed the sign for a slider. *Do not pitch a fastball.* Chrestler's slider was working. And the batter at the plate could knock a fastball out of the park.

If that happened, the Gems would hang up their cleats until spring. If not, the team would go to the World Series. Only one out away.

Don't think ahead. One game at a time.

If Chrestler threw a fastball, Tag would personally break a couple of the pitcher's fingers.

Chrestler released the ball. The hitter swung. The bat met the ball—loud as a firecracker—but not with the distinctive sound only made by the sweet spot on a maple bat connecting with cowhide. The batter had gotten under the pitch. Long fly ball. Leisurely sailing toward right field. The sole shooting star against the black backdrop of the nighttime sky.

The right fielder adjusted his cup and positioned his body for the catch. The play should have resulted in an easy out, but the ball smacked his glove before it bobbled to the grass.

The fans groaned, but Tag barely heard them. He focused on the punk who tagged up at second and headed for third. Tag threw off his mask and readied himself to protect home plate. Yep. The New York third-base coach was waving the punk home.

Shit, he was fast.

Tag stood directly behind the plate, silently cursing the rule change that prevented him from blocking the base. He wasn't taking any chances the out would be overturned because he'd messed up. Because he was going to make the out. Ensure his team would go to the World Series.

The ball rocketed in from right field. Punk's teeth flashed in a cocky grin the second before he went into his slide.

Tag stretched himself to catch the ball that was zooming toward him. The punk was sliding. Dust and chalk from the base path were like a jet contrail pluming behind him.

The ball landed in Tag's mitt, stinging his palm ever so slightly. He lunged forward, twisted ever so slightly, and tagged Punk's foot before it touched the base. The ump called the out.

Punk's cleats connected with the back of Tag's right knee where his leg guards didn't cover. Retracted ever so slightly, and then slammed the spot anew with the full force of Punk's body behind it.

It didn't matter. The game was over. The Columbia Gems had won the National League Pennant and were World Series bound.

Tag's teammates burst from the dugout and jumped him. Pounded his back. Danced around home plate. Fireworks exploded in the no-man's land behind the scoreboard, and a sulfuric stench from the gunpowder wafted into the stadium.

Tag's throat was dry from the billowing dust and all the whooping. He couldn't wait to get into the clubhouse and pop open the champagne management had on ice for just this occasion. It was sure going to taste mighty fine.

His teammates finally decided to let him up. He tried to stand.

His first clue something was wrong was the way his right leg wouldn't support him. The second indication was the pain that stole his breath and a sense of wetness. He hadn't been doused with the water bucket—that honor was reserved for the manager—so he looked down. And nearly puked.

Celeste Schuyler, Skye to her friends, wiped her brow with the back of her hand as she caught the end of the game on one of the many clubhouse monitors. The Gems winning the pennant was too good to be true. Skye's the Limit had a contract to cater the pregame clubhouse meals through the postseason. And she provided food to the luxury boxes, which would definitely be full for the World Series. Nobody had believed the Gems would go as far as they had, so she hadn't figured any postseason work into her schedule.

Tag Gentry's spectacular play had just guaranteed her at least two more jobs with the Gems this season. Work she needed to make the balloon payment due on her mortgage.

Not that Tag had won the game for her. Okay, so she had a little crush on him. Just a tiny one. Mostly because he flirted with her. She didn't read anything into his charming ways. She'd been feeding him before every home game since April, and he didn't even know her name.

"How about a kiss for luck, Red?" he'd ask before taking the field. Nope. He hadn't won this baseball game for her. He had no idea how desperately she needed the cash the additional games would bring.

She couldn't tear her attention from the silent monitor when she should have been scrubbing the steam table pans. The final out was being replayed. Skye was certain Tag's heroics would be analyzed to death over the next couple of days.

"Holy shit," someone said. "Tag Gentry is hurt."

Someone turned up the audio. Skye could see an amoeba stain of brilliant red oozing over the white uniform. None of the players bouncing on Tag seemed to notice until they decided to let him up.

Tag tried to stand. Most of the blood was coming from his knee.

"Oh!" Skye couldn't help the exclamation. Because there was more than a bloody knee wrong with Tag Gentry. Someone had ripped off his leg guards, revealing something like a tent pole bursting from his leg ...

Although her first instinct was to gag, Skye dropped her scouring pad into the pan and hurried to the lobby of the clubhouse, along with almost everyone else who wasn't on the field.

The standby ambulance team rushed through with a gurney. The monitors in the lobby showed the Gems falling away from Tag's supine body. Then the camera zoomed in as close as it could while the announcers spewed rampant speculation about the extent of Tag's injuries.

Skye turned away from the monitor to stare at the tunnel to the field. She cupped her right elbow in her left hand and chewed on her right thumbnail. Deep breaths didn't ease the tightness in her chest.

Security started clearing the lobby. Of course. The gurney carrying Tag would need unimpeded access to the ambulance.

Skye knew she should return to her cleaning up. Get back to her office and figure out what she'd need by way of supplies for the first two games of the World Series and how much closer to her dollar goal those two games would bring her.

The EMTs rushed through the tunnel. The rumble of the gurney wheels on the uneven concrete floor stopped Skye from returning to her task.

She couldn't help herself. She moved forward, wanting a better look at Tag.

His face was as white as the sheets concealing the hideous rearrangement of his leg. His eyes were closed, and his black lashes were stark against his skin.

Skye must have made some sort of sound because Tag opened his eyes. Homed in on her.

"Hey, Red. How about a kiss for luck?"

The EMTs rushed toward the ambulance.

"Hey guys, slow down," she heard him say as he whisked past her. "I need my good-luck kiss."

All season, Skye had ignored Tag's flirtatious invitation. He hadn't needed luck. The Gems had a phenomenal season and a miracle postseason.

"Hey, Red," Tag called as the gurney left the stadium. "You owe me one."

"I didn't realize you were...intimate with Gentry."

Skye turned to find Drake Dixon, majority shareholder of the Columbia Gems, standing behind her.

"I'm not. He likes to flirt." She didn't want Mr. Dixon to get the wrong idea. He had a huge say in whether or not her contract with the Gems would be renewed the following season. She knew he liked her food. He'd hired her to cater his upcoming Halloween party. But that didn't guarantee another contract with the Gems.

Mr. Dixon stepped closer. Too close. The miasma of his musk-laden cologne roiled in her stomach.

"Are the extra games going to create a problem for you?" he asked.

Skye forced a smile. "I'll make it work."

Some women might find Mr. Dixon attractive. Skye did not number among them. His eyes were too blue, his hair too golden, and his manner too suavely self-assured. His hands wandered too much. Like now. Reaching for her hand.

"Glad to know you're a team player."

A compound tibial shaft fracture. That was just the bone problem. The least of Tag's injuries. The New York punk had used his cleats to mangle some other stuff. Tag vaguely remembered hearing *"common fibular nerve, sural fascia, gastrocnemius"* and a couple of other anatomical terms. All he knew was his leg was messed up bad, and even though his play put his team in the World Series, he was staying home. He might get a championship ring out of ruining his leg. Some might say what he'd done was enough to earn one. But it wasn't the same thing. He'd been so close to the World Series. Yogi Berra was the only man in the history of baseball to catch a perfect World Series game, and Tag desperately wanted to be the second.

Fucking New York punk.

Just thinking about having to watch the Series from a hospital bed was enough to make Tag want to punch something. Like maybe one of the incessantly beeping monitors to which he was connected. He had money. His agent could negotiate with the team for home care. His penthouse was plenty big enough for whatever was needed.

Skye went over her ledger. If the Gems took the World Series to seven games—as they'd done with the championship series—she would be short only a few hundred dollars on her mortgage payment. There was one little problem: games six and seven would be played after the November first due date.

There was still Drake Dixon's Halloween party between now and her deadline, but as much as Dixon was paying her, it still wouldn't be quite enough.

If only there was a way to add another week or two to the calendar. Or at least to her grace period.

The only thing in life she ever wanted was a permanent home. Purchasing the old restaurant for her catering business had made sense at the time. So had the mortgage. But she must have been blinded by the stars in her eyes, because when the bank sent a reminder about the balloon payment, she'd been shocked.

Her cell phone buzzed at her elbow. The Gems' front office was calling, probably wanting to confirm the dates and times of the first two games of the World Series.

"Skye's the Limit. Skye speaking."

She listened. She doodled. She listened some more.

Tag Gentry was home from the hospital and needed someone to provide meals for him. The team wanted to hire her to feed him. And someone was going to pay her a whole lot of money to do so.

How could she turn down the job?

She couldn't. The player being Tag Gentry meant nothing. She was professional enough not to let her little crush interfere with doing the job.

Maybe she'd just been granted a miracle.

Thank God he wasn't stuck in a rehab center.

Team management wanted Tag in a professional facility. Tag even understood why. But he had most of the equipment he'd needed right in his workout room in his penthouse. The physical therapist could damn well come to him. He was the hero of the moment. A little gratitude was in order.

Either way, he was going to go nuts. He called his current lady friend, but she was out of the country. Terra Baldwin was a reporter for a cable news network and was always running off to the far corners of the globe in search of a story.

"I'm in Wheretheheckistan," she'd told him. *"I heard rumors the government was going to test a nuclear weapon."*

That was his Terra. Always on an adventure. No wonder they got along so well. When they saw each other. It had been a while. He could have used a little female company while he was grounded.

His chest was so tight it hurt to breathe. He should be at the stadium, taking batting practice, working with the bullpen. He needed to be with his team. The backup catcher was okay, but he wasn't World Series ready.

The Gems were so fucked.

He said as much to his agent when Marty called.

"They know that. And you're fucked anyway, so quit stressing." Marty Fiscoe was not a coddler. "Your physical therapist is coming to your place. Any equipment you don't have, they'll order in."

"The team's paying, right?"

"I'm still working on that. The team would have paid for the rehab facility. Moving the facility to your place might be a different song. You've got a day nurse and night nurse coming in, and your meals will be brought in by the team caterer."

Tag didn't need taking care of. He needed something to do.

Or so he thought, until his physical therapist, a Bluto clone, showed up. The guy was a sadist. Tag reminded him about the tibial whatever bone sticking out through his skin, but Bluto didn't seem to give a shit.

Neither did the day nurse. A guy. Who looked vaguely familiar. Like Hans, from old seasons of *Saturday Night Live.* And so Tag dubbed the male night nurse Franz.

When did men start being nurses? Tag had been hoping for a busty blonde, but the way his luck had been going, Tag could have gotten stuck with Nurse Ratched.

He tried to convince himself the testosterone was good for his recovery. There were only four months until pitchers and catchers had to report for spring training, and Dr. Jekyll, also known as Dr. Jackson, had warned Tag he might not be ready. His injuries were too severe.

Concentrate on getting better. Don't get distracted.

Franz opened the door for the caterer.

Red. Tag's pulse jumpstarted. "You here to give me that kiss for luck you owe me?"

She smiled. "Nope. I'm here to feed you."

"Man food, I hope."

"Healing food," Red replied.

He'd never paid much attention to the team caterer, other than her hair and asking her for a kiss before every home game. It was just something he did. Completely harmless.

He stopped his wheelchair in the door of the kitchen and watched her unload packages onto his counter.

"I didn't know what kind of kitchen setup you had, so I made everything for the next twenty-four hours microwavable." She didn't look at him as she unloaded the contents of her rolling cooler into his refrigerator. "Tonight's supper, tomorrow's breakfast, lunch, and a couple of snacks. The heating instructions are written on the containers."

"I can't reach the microwave," he said. He didn't bother mentioning his limited access to the fridge. "I guess Franz will have to do the reheating."

Faint color stained her cheeks. "I didn't realize you had someone with you, so I didn't prepare enough food—"

"Franz can order up a pizza," Tag said.

"I'll make enough food for two tomorrow."

"Don't worry about it, Red."

"Skye."

"Huh?"

"My name is Skye. I own Skye's the Limit Catering."

"Red Skye at night, a catcher's delight." He thought he was pretty clever.

Her lips—very nice lips—parted. "That is...stupid."

Red's entire face fascinated him. He'd never noticed her eyes before. They weren't green, and they weren't blue but a cross somewhere between the two colors. Like the tropical lagoon where he had swum with sharks.

"Stay awhile and keep me company."

"I can't. Besides, you've got your night nurse."

"Franz?" Tag snorted. "He's here to make sure I don't fall if I need to whiz in the middle of the night."

The color in her cheeks deepened. "Try playing cards with him. I hear you're good at pitch."

"I'm good with pitchers. Pay attention, Red."

She zipped the top of her rolling cooler. "I'll see you tomorrow. Let me know if you have any requests. You can have anything that was on the regular menu at the clubhouse."

She headed toward the front door. The denim of her jeans clung to her nicely shaped ass.

"I don't have your number."

"Your night nurse has my business card."

And she was gone. Just like that.

Tag pulled his phone from his pocket and looked up Skye's the Limit Catering. He liked what he read. Celeste Schuyler specialized in sports nutrition and vegetarian cuisine. He wouldn't have recognized her from the photo on her website. Her kinky copper-colored hair was down—something he'd never seen. She was smiling too. A big, all-encompassing grin. God, if she ever smiled at him like that, he wouldn't be responsible for his actions.

He dialed the number on the website.

"Skye's the Limit Catering. Skye speaking."

"Hey, Red. Who the hell named you Celeste?"

"Hello, Tag."

"How'd you know it was me?"

"You're the only one who calls me Red."

At least she didn't sound annoyed. "So you specialize in sports nutrition. Who else uses you besides the Gems?"

"Athletes who demand too much from their bodies."

"Hey. This was not my fault. All I was doing was catching a ball. Blame that punk from New York. I do. Every second of every minute since he slid into my knee and slammed me with his cleats."

"You can heat the chicken breast in the microwave."

"You already said that, and I already told you I can't reach the microwave. Can I have a steak tomorrow night? I could really go for a grilled top sirloin. Bring enough for Franz and yourself, and we'll have a little party. We could open a bottle of wine, but alcohol and my meds don't mix. At least, that's what the doctor said. But you could drink. Maybe I could get you drunk and have my wicked way with you."

"Let me see what I can do for you and Franz. Find out what he likes so I can take that into consideration when I'm buying supplies."

"So, do you like baseball or football better?" Tag asked quickly, before she could disconnect on him.

"What?"

He worked his way to his recliner. He never thought there'd be a time when sitting was preferable to action. "Do you like football or baseball better? Or maybe basketball. Who's easier to feed?"

He heard a sigh. Or something.

"I'll see what I can do about a steak tomorrow night. Find out what your night nurse wants and e-mail or text me."

"What about Hans and Bluto?"

"What?"

"Do we have a bad connection or something? You keep asking me to repeat myself. I asked about my day nurse and physical therapist. They need to eat too."

"Your nurses are Hans and Franz, and your physical therapist is Bluto?"

"You got a problem with that?"

"Find out what they want and text me. I'm hanging up now, Tag." And she did.

He resisted the urge to call her back. He was going to have way too much time to get to know her. Getting to know her better would at least give him something to do.

Skye fumed as she unlocked the back door of Skye's the Limit. The alley was dark except for the halo created by the security light over the door. The lock was sticky. Replacing it was on the top of her list. Right after the balloon payment.

Which she'd better be able to make after all the nonsense the Gems were putting her through. Nobody had warned her Tag Gentry was high maintenance. And nobody had said a word about feeding his team of caretakers when they'd hired her to nursemaid him. Hans, Franz, and Bluto, indeed. What name would he come with for her?

Oh. He already had: Red.

She could feed Tag and gang from the same meals she was prepping for game one of the World Series. Then she could start on the appetizers for Drake Dixon's Halloween bash. Right on schedule.

Oh, and she needed to call the bank to ask about a slight extension on her balloon payment due date. A week would do it. But bank business had to wait until morning. In the meantime, she would start boiling eggs for Halloween Devils.

She filled her pot with water and set it on the front burner of the stove that had come with the building. Someday she was going to replace the ancient monstrosity with a double convection oven, six-burner, grill, and flat top all-in-one unit. After the balloon payment. And the lock change.

She turned the knob and waited for the faint *whoosh* of the gas igniting. Nothing. She peered under the pot. No blue flame licked at the copper bottom.

Damn. The burners were working less and less frequently, no matter how often she scoured the burner rings. She'd need to light the pilot manually with a kitchen match. After moving the pot of water to the counter, she removed the burner grates from all six burners and then raised the top of the range. Not one of the three pilots was lit, which explained the faint aroma of cooking gas lingering in the room. All three pilots had never extinguished at the same time before. That concerned her. As did the scent of gas.

Maybe she should call the utility company. They wouldn't charge her to check for a gas leak.

And they didn't. Nor did they charge her to shut off the gas to the building. The incoming lines were fine. The lines inside the building were fine. The ancient monstrosity of a stove was not. No gas also meant no hot water.

The time she should have spent negotiating with the bank the next morning was instead spent calling appliance repair businesses, who wanted at least a hundred and eighty dollars just to make a house call. Only to tell her the stove was unsalvageable.

Without a stove, she was sunk. Without a stove, she wouldn't need the building, and all the money she'd already poured into architectural drawings and renovating the old restaurant into a cozy catering facility would be lost.

Unless she could find someplace else to...

Tag Gentry. He had a big, sterile, and underutilized kitchen. The place looked as if it had been designed for a magazine, with its restaurant stove, double-size subzero stainless-steel refrigerator, and marble counters. He needed meals, and the Gems were paying her to feed him. Nobody except the state said where she had to prep those meals. Okay, maybe Hans, Franz, and Bluto might not like her being there, and if the Health Department ever found out...but she had to do something.

Skye's the Limit wasn't the building. It was her. Where she prepped her meals didn't matter, except for her kosher clients. But Passover was months away. She had a more immediate problem, and Tag Gentry's kitchen could be her salvation.

October 25, World Series Game 1

When Skye arrived at Tag's apartment that afternoon, he was in a physical therapy session. Hans, the day nurse, let her in.

"Great lunch and breakfast. Thanks." He did look a little like Dana Carvey. "If you're doing all the cooking, this job isn't going to be so bad."

"Glad you enjoyed it." Skye pushed her rolling cart toward the kitchen.

"I thought you weren't coming back until tonight," Hans said as he followed her.

"Change of plan." She didn't have to explain anything to him.

The first haul from her van involved her baking sheets and other kitchen tools she simply could not work without. At least for what was on her agenda for the day. She'd bring over her other equipment as she needed it.

Next came the giant coolers with the produce she'd purchased from the market at dawn. Before her stove had been pronounced dead. By the time she'd finished unloading the van, Tag was done with his PT session. Hans was helping him shower.

Skye tied on her apron and went to work. First up: marinate the giant portabella mushrooms before she grilled them. Yes, Tag had a built-in grill in the kitchen, so food prep was that much simpler. Gluten-free pasta with grilled portabella mushroom slices and a fresh bruschetta-style marinara would be the main entrée for the Gems. A side of dark healthy greens tossed with a citrusy dressing completed the meal, which was one of the team's favorites. Making it before game one of the World Series was a good-luck gesture on her part.

"What the hell are you doing?"

Skye jumped. She'd been so intent on chiffonading basil leaves, she hadn't heard Tag wheel into the kitchen. Black stubble covered the lower half of his face. His dark hair was still damp on his forehead and curled in j's as if a stuttering computer keyboard had gone berserk. Deep grooves bracketed his eyes and mouth, hinting at the pain he had to be in.

"Fixing your dinner," she replied as she applied her knife to the bundle of herbs. Better to focus on her work than on his biceps—which were exposed by a gray tank top—or the heavily muscled thighs revealed by his gray sweat shorts. More dark hair curled on his one exposed calf.

Not that she'd noticed.

"I don't eat that much," he said.

She glanced at him and saw his stare fixed on the giant pot of water she'd put to boil on the back burner of his stove.

"I thought I'd save time and prep the team's meal while I made yours."

He narrowed his eyes, which were the same cold gray as the stainless-steel refrigerator door. "Isn't it a little bizarre to be cooking for the team in my kitchen?"

Skye shrugged to hide her discomfort. She could pull this off. She had to pull it off. "The team hero deserves the freshest meal I can serve him."

"Don't call me that." The steel was in his voice too.

Skye turned to face him, keeping her knife in her hand. "If you hadn't covered home base the way you did—"

"If they hadn't changed the frigging rules so I couldn't block the plate, that punk never would have caught me with his cleats."

"Or his cleats could have caught you in a more vulnerable spot."

TAG WANTED TO snort. There wasn't a more vulnerable spot on a catcher's body except his balls. A guy's cup could protect him, even though it would still hurt like hell. But he wasn't about to enlighten the caterer.

Who looked as if she'd moved into his kitchen. Mounds of multicolored vegetables covered the counter near the sink. A deep pot he knew damned well wasn't his teetered on a back burner of the stove he was positive had never been used before.

She wielded a big-ass knife with flecks of dark green stuff clinging to the blade. The room smelled like pesto.

"Let me clarify my question. What the hell are you doing in my kitchen?"

He was in pain from his PT session. The last thing in the world he wanted was another stranger knocking around his apartment. Hans and Bluto—he didn't have a choice. But Red?

This was taking flirtation to a level he didn't want to visit. At least not right now. Maybe in a couple of weeks when he was feeling better and his leg had healed. Not now. Not with Pain and Torture on the agenda twice a day.

"The Gems hired me to prepare your meals, along with the team's meals for the duration of the postseason."

"They didn't rent my kitchen for you to do your thing."

Her magic. She served the best pregame meals he'd ever tasted.

"I'm trying to save myself some time here." Red sounded exasperated, when he was the one with every right to be annoyed. "The Gems aren't my only client, and I hadn't planned on feeding you and your...staff."

She snapped at him. Red actually had the audacity to snap at him because she was trespassing in his apartment.

And she wasn't finished. "It's not as if you're using your kitchen. There isn't even a Chinese take-out menu hanging from a pizza delivery magnet on your refrigerator door."

"Don't judge me."

"I'm trying to feed you."

He needed to eat. He didn't need any more grief. "Fine." Stomping off in a wheelchair didn't have the same impact.

Skye sagged against the counter. She'd managed. At least for one day

She delivered the food to the stadium on time. The players dug in. There was a new tension in the clubhouse. Excitement hummed. The World Series. Every baseball team dreamed of reaching this moment.

"Good food, Skye," a couple of guys said, but mostly they ate in intense silence.

She usually hung around to watch the game, but she couldn't afford to take the time this night. She hurried through cleanup, packed the leftovers for the local homeless shelter, and left before the second inning started.

Drake Dixon stopped her on her way out to tell her he was changing the date of his Halloween party from Saturday to Monday because the Gems would be playing game four of the Series on Saturday. He didn't want to be distracted. And Monday *was* Halloween. And a travel date, should the Gems not wrap up the Series in four or five games.

"I hope that's not a problem."

"Not at all," Skye lied. Postponing the party meant delaying his payment, which she might not receive by November first. She smiled anyway.

He bumped knuckles with her clenched fist. "How's it going with Gentry?"

"Fine." As if she'd admit to anything else.

"Well, I won't keep you any longer."

"Good night, Mr. Dixon."

She drove to Skye's the Limit to pick up the dozens of eggs she needed to boil for Dixon's party.

The heaviness in her chest as she surveyed the kitchen hindered her breathing. How many years had she dreamed of her own place? Since her mother's death when Skye was eight? That was when her unsuccessful salesman father started dragging her from town to town as he bounced from job to job. Skye craved stability.

Her father had never appreciated her homemaking efforts. A few wildflowers stuck in an empty olive jar earned her a sneer. If he noticed at all. A nicely cooked meal was shoveled down as hurriedly as canned spaghetti. And every few months, when he'd lost yet another job, Skye would pack up their sparse belongings and wish for roots.

Her father had died the week before her eighteenth birthday. She missed him. He was her father. He'd done his best by her. But she was finally free to escape his nightmare and follow her own dreams. Columbia, South Carolina, was a good place to start. Hard work had landed her the catering job with the Gems.

Business was good and growing. She already had one part-time employee and had been thinking about adding another once she paid off the building.

Now it was time to regroup. She had plenty of practice doing that.

And whether he knew it or not, Tag Gentry was going to help her.

Someone like Tag wouldn't understand how growing up without a base had formed the way she thought. He was secure in his traditional nuclear family—according to the team's official bio. Yeah. She'd checked. Little crush, not stalking. He'd had a mother, father, and numerous siblings. He'd never had to wonder where he'd be sleeping. Never had to wonder if the roof would leak or where he'd be in relation to the rest of his class when he started yet another new school. His kind of cocky confidence would carry him wherever he wanted to go.

Not everyone in the world was that self-assured. But she was learning. And somehow, she was going to survive the dead stove and the balloon payment.

November first. Seven days.

October 26, World Series Game 2

Damned if Red wasn't in his kitchen when he got out of his post-PT shower the next morning. Cooking for game two of the Series. Or so she claimed.

Tag had stayed up to watch the first game. The night nurse didn't like baseball, so he'd busied himself elsewhere. Tag was tempted to ask for another nurse. What kind of man didn't like baseball?

Someone should have been watching the game with him. A guy shouldn't have to watch his team play an important game alone. The Gems won, but there was no one to exchange high fives with. His tribe was on the field. His sometimes woman was chasing nuclear bombs half a world away.

Tag wheeled his chair into the kitchen, where he'd be in Red's way as she worked.

"So did you stay at the stadium to watch the game?" He had no idea what her usual routine was. He'd see her on his way out to the field before a game and ask for a kiss. That was all he knew about her.

"Not last night. I have a big Halloween party I'm getting ready for. I hadn't planned on the Gems doing so well in the postseason." Red did something with pieces of raw chicken, plastic wrap, and a big wooden hammer.

"You're supposed to believe in your team."

"My bad." She whacked the chicken with the hammer. "Sue me. Let me warn you. There's a line."

"You don't need to get all hostile on me. Especially since you're using my kitchen rent-free."

"I was hired to feed you. I'm cooking for you." Another piece of chicken underwent suffocation in plastic wrap.

"You're a caterer. You bring food in."

"I brought food in. And now I'm cooking it." She dropped the chicken she'd just pounded the hell out of onto a tray already piled with other pieces of chicken. "Grilled chicken and vegetables. You love it."

"I told you I wanted steak."

"Tomorrow."

"It's my kitchen. I get to decide the menu."

Red dropped her hammer and glared at him. "What is your problem? I'm not blocking access to your refrigerator where you keep your beer. And I'm pretty sure you're not supposed to have beer anyway."

Tag narrowed his eyes. "I want to know why you've invaded my kitchen. I never invited you to hang out at my place."

Red snorted. "What are you worried about? I'll find out all your secrets? I've got news for you. You have no secrets. This apartment has all the personality of a cheap motel room."

"What do you know about cheap motel rooms?" For some reason, that image bothered him.

"I have a problem at my building right now, and rather than renege on my contract with the Gems, I thought I would use your fabulous kitchen to honor my commitments. Do you have an issue with that?"

Her fierceness surprised him. "You could have asked. Before you moved in knife, hammer, and cake pans."

"I didn't think you'd notice." Red averted her gaze and picked up the wooden hammer again. Started abusing another slab of chicken. *Thwack.* "I thought you'd be so busy with your physical therapy and feeling sorry for yourself, you'd never notice someone in your kitchen. Heck, I would have bet you didn't even know you had a kitchen."

"Beer in the fridge," he reminded her in a dry tone. He was starting to get an idea. "What kind of problems are you having at your building?"

"Just problems."

He knew an evasion when he heard one. "Vermin? Plumbing? Roof leaking?" It hadn't rained in weeks.

"Check, check, check." *Thwack.*

"Sounds dire." He couldn't keep a glimmer of amusement out of his tone.

Thwack. Thwack. "More dire than you can imagine."

"Life or death?"

"Life. Mine, anyway." She bit her lower lip, and he envied her teeth.

"I have a proposition for you." He was probably going to regret this, but he really didn't want to watch the game alone a second night. Or a third.

She looked at him, hammer paused midair. "I don't put out."

If he'd been drinking something, he would have choked. "In case you haven't noticed, I'm not exactly in any kind of shape to show you a good time, much less a great one."

"Well, that's a relief." *Thwack!*

A relief? He must be losing his touch. Women lined up to get Tagged.

"If you come back here tonight after you're done in the clubhouse and watch the game, you can use my kitchen."

"What?" She pulled the plastic wrap from the chicken she'd just mutilated.

"Are you hearing impaired, or do I mumble? I know you watch baseball. You can watch the World Series with me."

"I don't watch baseball. I follow the Gems."

"Newsflash, Red. The Gems are a baseball team."

She rolled those lagoon-colored eyes. "I need to see how you guys perform and make adjustments to your menus."

"Never more crucial a time than during the World Series. You can watch the game here just as well as you can watch from…wherever."

"I have to work. The team isn't my only customer. I have this enormous Halloween party coming up—"

"I just said you could use my kitchen."

"I'm already using your kitchen." Another piece of chicken found itself smothered in plastic and then beaten with her wooden hammer.

"Without my permission," he reminded her. "Look, I just want someone as invested in the team winning as I am to watch with me. Is it too much to ask?"

"No." Her voice was low. "I guess I could do that. It's a fair trade."

At least Skye didn't have to sneak her equipment into Tag's empty cupboards. He even put Hans to work helping her unload her van. Fortunately, all those years of moving around the country with her father had given her skills in setting up her workspace in a new kitchen quickly and efficiently.

Tag left her alone the rest of the afternoon.

Grilled chicken with veggies was a team favorite, so cleanup was a breeze. She arrived at Tag's place in record time. She let herself in with the key Tag had given her.

"Where have you been? It's already the third inning." Tag sounded as petulant as a child as he shouted from the living room.

"Cleaning up. Dropping off the leftovers at the homeless shelter on Montrose."

Being waylaid by Drake Dixon again and suffering a victory hug from him.

"What?"

"Are you hard of hearing, or do I mumble?"

"I'm distracted by the game. Come on. Javi is at bat."

Skye had gotten to know most of the team on a superficial level, and she would rank Javier Rodriguez as an arrogant ass. If she were a pitcher in the National League, she would work on her batting skills. Not Rodriguez. He racked up more strikeouts at the plate than he threw from the mound.

"I can't stand watching him humiliate himself," Skye said as she headed for the kitchen.

"We have a deal, you and me."

"Right." She changed directions.

She could work on deviling Dixon's eggs tomorrow, which was a travel day. Her only obligation besides feeding Tag was prepping for Halloween.

At least Tag's TV wasn't in his bedroom. The screen was huge and mounted on the living room wall. A black leather recliner claimed the best spot. Burgundy leather sofas formed an L to the left of the recliner. A card table, laden with snacks and a small cooler, sat to Tag's right.

"Why are you eating that crap?" Skye asked. The nutritionist in her was seriously annoyed.

"Shh." Tag gestured with his beverage at the screen. "It's what Franz put out for me."

"It's more like what you had Franz buy for you." She knew the large loaded pizza and tub of hot wings hadn't been in the apartment when she left.

"Sit and watch."

Half the pizza was gone. Wing bones played a game of Jenga on a paper plate.

"Didn't I leave enough dinner for you?"

"Franz doesn't like his vegetables."

"Where is Franz?"

"I don't know. He gets paid to watch me, not the other way around. Damn it, Javi. Don't you know a sinker from a slider?"

"Rodriguez doesn't know his elbow from a hole in the ground," Skye said. She started clearing the food off the table.

"Hey! I need to eat."

"Not this stuff. I'll fix you something better."

"The pizza has vegetables on it. There's red and green peppers, onions, and mushrooms."

"For Franz?"

Tag grinned. "Busted. He liked the grilled stuff you left so much, he ate it all. Didn't leave a bite for me."

"You're so full of baloney, your eyes ought to be pink," she said. "Part of healing involves good nutrition. I thought you wanted to report to spring training come February."

"Mom, it's the World Series. It's party time."

Skye shook her head. She took the pizza to the kitchen and wrapped each slice in foil before refrigerating it.

"You better not be tossing my pizza!" Tag yelled.

Skye waited until she was in the living room, packing up the wings to respond. "Moderation. I'm saving your junk for the next game."

Tag snickered. "Is that a come-on, Red? Because I already told you. You're gonna have to wait to be Tagged."

Skye's face heated. "You are such a guy."

"What else am I supposed to be? A porpoise?"

Skye fled with the wings. She puttered in the kitchen. She was reluctant to be alone with him. He was funny. Fun to be with. Not good for her crush.

"Come on, Red. Pay your rent. It's the middle of the fourth."

She returned to the living room with a bowl of green and red grapes. "You're snacking because you're nervous," she said as she handed him the bowl. "Eat these instead."

He stared at the bowl as if he'd never seen a grape before. "Seriously?"

"They'll crunch for you. You need to trust me."

"That's what Bluto said. He's a sadist. But you're cuter."

"No flirting with the caterer." Skye plopped on the end of the sofa as far from Tag's recliner as she could get.

He didn't say anything until the commercial break between the fourth and fifth innings. "I could go for a beer."

"You can't go anywhere. You should be in a rehab facility."

"You could get me a beer."

"It's not on your plan for this week. You're taking some pretty potent meds. You should be getting enough of a buzz from them."

"You are such a spoilsport."

"I'm not a sport at all. I'm a cook."

"Yeah, you're a good cook. Gems have the best pregame meals in the league."

"Thank you. You still can't have a beer."

The Gems had a two-run lead going into the ninth. Skye was familiar enough with the game to know two wins before hitting the road was a good thing.

The game went downhill in the top of the inning. Adam Chrestler came in as the closing pitcher.

Tag started grumbling. "Wes doesn't know how to work with Chrestler." Wes was Wesley Dornan, the backup catcher. "You gotta be firm with Chrestler. He thinks nobody can hit his fastball, and that's a fantasy."

The first batter hit a grounder to short, but the throw to first wasn't in time. Seattle had a runner on base.

"Slider," Tag muttered at the television. "Don't let Chrestler shake you off."

The camera zoomed in on Wes's white-painted fingernails he flashed signs between his splayed thighs.

"Not a fucking sinker!" Tag screamed. "Not to this guy!"

Skye glanced at Tag. He needed to keep his blood pressure down.

The crack of the bat drew her gaze back to the big screen just as Tag blistered her ears with his extensive vocabulary of curses.

"Calm down." She vaguely heard the announcer say something about a sweet spot and good-bye. The ball sailed over the right field wall and into the stands.

"You saw that! Stupid kid told Chrestler to throw a sinker. Chrestler's sinker is more hittable than his fastball! And this batter... Didn't Wes do his homework? Everybody knows Wilson can knock a sinker out of the park."

"If you don't chill, I'm going to get Franz and make him tranq you." She probably had more riding on this game than Tag, but she wasn't going ballistic.

"I wouldn't try it," Tag snapped.

"Pay attention to your game. It looks like we missed the first out."

Tag started swearing again, ending with, "I need to call that kid and tell him how to do his homework on the hitters."

"You can't call him during the game." She needed to distract him before he popped a blood vessel. "Now tell me what's going on."

"We blew a two-run lead."

Skye narrowed her eyes. "Really? I never would have guessed."

Tag returned the glare. "Sarcasm isn't attractive."

"Good thing I'm not trying to attract you. Now look at the screen and tell me what's going on."

"Tie game. Nobody on base. One out. Guy at the plate used to play for Florida. He's an inside pitch hitter. Best pitch to nail him is a curveball, but Chrestler doesn't have one. Not even a bad one."

"So what is Wes signaling him to do?"

"Are you spying for Seattle?"

Skye rolled her eyes. "Not when the Gems pay me by the home game."

"If we lose this game—"

"It's not over until it's over," she reminded him. "And there's no crying in baseball, so suck it up. What's Wes telling Chrestler to do?"

"Slider. Chrestler's slider is a thing of beauty. If I could write poetry, I 'd write a poem to it."

The Gems got out of the inning with no further damage.

Bottom of the ninth, tie game, and Tag wasn't there to help his team. His absence could very well be the reason the game was tied. If he'd been there to handle Chrestler, they wouldn't need to go to the bottom of the ninth.

He reached for a peanut. Popped it into his mouth, intent on the screen, forgetting her substitution until he bit down and sweet grape juice flooded his tongue. Stupid woman food.

"What did you do with my nuts?" That came out wrong.

Red ignored him, and he didn't blame her.

"My mixed nuts. Nuts are healthy."

"In moderation," she replied. "Which is a concept I believe you're unfamiliar with."

"Moderation didn't get the Gems to the World Series," he snapped.

She simply looked at him. Her eyes held an expression he wasn't familiar with, so he could only guess what it was. He didn't like the answer.

No one pitied Tag Gentry.

The commercial break ended. The announcers recapped the bottom of the eighth. Tag knew he had to divert Red's attention before the moment grew maudlin.

"Hey, Red. How about a kiss for luck?"

She shocked the shit out of him when she scooted off the couch and planted one on him. Not his forehead. Not his cheek. His mouth. The press of her lips against his shot a bolt of heat directly to his groin.

"Now watch the game." She'd already returned to the couch. Out of reach.

Right. The game.

But it was difficult to focus when he had a boner that felt like the size of Chrestler's bat. And nothing ever distracted him from the game. Ever.

Chrestler was up and down on three pitches. The top of the order was next.

The first baseman's postseason hitting streak continued with a line drive to center, which put the winning run on first base.

Tag tried to sit forward, but the bundle on his leg didn't allow for much movement. The shortstop sent a sac fly to center, advancing the runner to second.

Tubby Maldonado came to the plate. He was a big guy. If he could get his weight behind the bat, he was capable of knocking the ball to the moon. He also had a knack for swinging at bad pitches. His grin flashed white against his deeply tanned face. It was not a pleasant grin. Tag had seen him practice it in the mirror.

But Tubby was on. He waited out a curve ball that was nowhere near the outside edge of the plate. And a second one. The next curve ball was so inside it could have trimmed inches off Tubby's gut had he not jumped out of the batter's box.

The next ball sailed over the center of the base until Tubby's bat collided with it. The crack was different on TV than live, but Tag recognized the sound: sweet spot against cowhide.

Tag started to leap from his chair. His roar of victory turned to a yelp of pain.

"Are you okay?" Red was at his side immediately. "Do you need me to call Franz?"

Tag blinked back the wetness the unexpected jostle had put in his eyes. "Gimme another kiss," he replied. He grasped her arms and pulled her into his lap. "You kissed me for luck, and it worked. Now kiss me to make it better."

He didn't give her a chance to reply.

Her lips were as tender as new spring grass in right field. And she tasted sweet—sweeter than the stupid grapes she'd substituted for his nuts. The shock of pain in his leg when he'd moved wrong was nothing compared to the jolt of lust aimed straight at his dick as his tongue parted Red's lips. Her bottom was pliable too, unlike Terra's or any of the other women with whom he usually fucked. And surprisingly, he liked soft.

Red pushed at his shoulders.

Whoa.

He relaxed his grip. She catapulted off his lap. Her face was pale. Her lagoon eyes were wide and stormy. Her mouth was wet from his. Her lips were pink and puffy.

"We won." His voice was hoarse. "How about a high five?"

Red turned her back and left the room.

If he had two good legs, he never would have let her get away with ignoring him. If he had two good legs, maybe she'd be under him, naked and accepting him in her body as a celebration of the two-game lead the Gems had before going on the road.

If he had two good legs, he wouldn't even be stuck in his apartment with her. He'd be in the clubhouse, celebrating with his team.

He clicked off the TV.

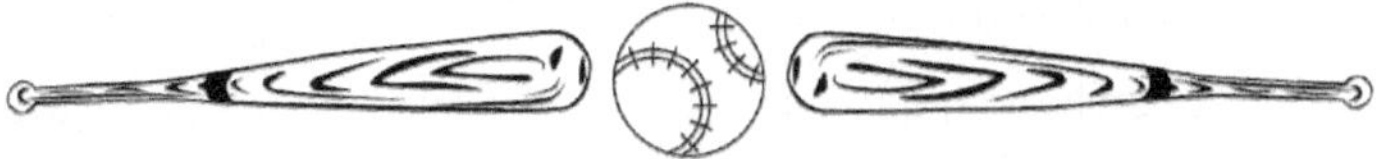

Skye pulled out her largest mixing bowl and started measuring dry ingredients into it. Her brain was numb. Unlike the rest of her body, which was still vibrating from Tag's touch. The first kiss had been devastating enough, but that second kiss, the one in his lap...

She gulped in air and tried to focus on her cake recipe. Baking usually soothed her. But her hands shook. Her stomach knotted. Her backside was branded with the imprint of Tag Gentry's erection.

She dropped her spoon and gripped the edge of the marble counter while the kitchen spun around her.

Okay. The Gems had won their game. Winning meant everything to guys like Tag, whose livelihood depended on winning. He was just excited because his team needed to put away only two more games to be world champions. She just happened to be there.

Because he wanted her there. Her presence was his price for letting her use his kitchen. *"Watch the game with me."* And she'd agreed. But not to being mauled afterward.

Even if she liked it. A little. Because of her minor crush. But she had more respect for herself than that. She was handy. Franz probably wasn't a very good kisser, and he'd been quite vocal about not giving a damn about the outcome of the baseball game, whereas she cared about the outcome.

She cracked a couple of eggs into the bowl.

She'd been handy. That was all. She deserved more than being the breathing equivalent of a handkerchief.

What would you have to lose?

She was already teetering on the edge of disaster. Pulling down her panties for Tag Gentry might be the nudge that completed her destruction.

Vanilla splashed into the bowl, dripping from her measuring spoon.

Damn it all, I'm a professional. I worked a whole season surrounded by hot baseball players and never once crossed the line between fan girl and mature adult. It was a kiss. Only a kiss.

Tag wasn't the only player to attempt to play her, but she'd laughed them off as being teases and kept things light. Until Tag had been injured, she'd even ignored her crush as thoroughly as she ignored his plea for a good-luck kiss.

Being in his apartment—maybe that was the difference. She'd looked at the sterile place and seen nothing of what she expected the man to be. Maybe this was what he considered home. The furnishings belonged to him. And now she was one of the kitchen appliances.

And she planned to stay that way: unused by occupant.

October 27, World Series Travel Day

S kye started her day arguing with the bank about the due date of her balloon payment. Their stubborn refusal to budge even one minute was what turned the conversation from a negotiation to an argument.

"I would think you would want a late payment rather than a foreclosure." But reason wasn't working. "I will even pay you a late fee. That will make you money. A foreclosure will cost you."

It was as if she hadn't reached a real person at all but rather just another "Press One for Dead End" option on the bank's voice mail system. As far as Skye could tell, there wasn't a difference.

She'd call again tomorrow. Maybe she'd be connected to someone with a heart.

She tucked her phone into her pocket and glanced around Skye's the Limit's kitchen. Dust motes drifted in the slant of sunlight creeping through the louvered shutters. The counters looked bare without the usual jumble of produce, small appliances, and meals-in-progress.

Tag's kitchen was nice, but it wasn't hers. Here, she didn't even need to think because everything was set up exactly the way her mind worked while she was cooking. Yes, she'd taken her own tools to Tag's place and his major appliances were restaurant quality, but the layout hadn't been designed with a working cook in mind.

A knock on the back door startled her out of her reverie.

She couldn't imagine who would be there. As far as most people knew, the building was empty. She'd done nothing with the restaurant front except cover the windows so no one could peek in. The back door, the one to the kitchen, was in an alley, not a street. There was no walk-in traffic. She didn't even have an index card tacked to the door announcing her business. The people who knew her would have called before dropping by. Few people knew she lived on the third floor of the building. She hadn't reached the point of success where regular deliveries of anything were scheduled. Her business came from her website and referrals.

A knock on the back door at nine thirty in the morning was...unusual.

And yeah, repairing the doorbell was on the replacing-the-lock line of her strategic plan.

Skye peered through a gap in the shutter. Her stomach lurched, and her breath hung up on her tonsils for a moment. Drake Dixon.

She tried to remember if she'd brushed her teeth yet that morning. Her hair was down, as she wasn't working on food prep yet, and it needed to dry from her cold shower. The only meals on the agenda for the day were for Tag and his entourage. The rest of the day was devoted to prep for Dixon's Halloween party. And here he was. Outside her kitchen.

He knocked again.

Skye wiped her hands on the front of her jeans.

"Mr. Dixon. What brings you around here this morning?" she asked as she opened the door. Her smile felt phony and awkward.

"Good morning, Skye." He stood a little too close, so she stepped back, which he apparently mistook as an invitation to enter.

The kitchen had passed the Health Department's last inspection, but it didn't have the shiny, stainless steel look a lot of customers might think it should have. Skye wasn't ashamed of the space. She just didn't want to have to defend it.

She walked around to the far side of the produce prep island and propped her elbows on the wooden surface. "What brings you around this morning?"

He smiled. Smarmy. A mild excuse for the clenching of her stomach. "You seemed a touch stressed last night when we spoke, and I wondered if the change of date really was a problem."

"No. Really. It's not. It actually gives me more time to work on it."

"Do you need an advance to purchase supplies?"

Skye swallowed. Forced a noncommittal smile to curve her mouth. "No. Supplies are all set. In fact, I've already started a couple of things. But thanks."

What was he doing there? How did he even know where she based her business? Her advertising listed only her cell phone number, her website, and other social media contact information. His presence was more than a little creepy.

"Business is good?" He settled on the stool across from her.

"Yes. Besides the baseball games and your party, I have an election-night party on the books and the Jaycees' Harvest Ball. Oh, and one of the players hired me to cater his wedding on Thanksgiving weekend." The work was there. If the health codes, zoning ordinances, and building association didn't catch up with her. Using Tag's kitchen had to be breaking all kinds of regulations.

"And Tag Gentry."

"Feeding Tag isn't quite the scope of the other jobs." He was more like feeding...a boyfriend. Not that she would admit that to Mr. Dixon. And she probably would have taken on the job for free. Something else Dixon didn't need to know.

Dixon reached across the island and placed his hand over hers. His skin was cool and paper dry. Or maybe hers was overheated.

"Don't work too hard. I wouldn't want my favorite caterer to exhaust herself."

The man had a line. She would have to give him that.

"Don't worry. I won't."

He lingered a few more minutes before leaving.

After she closed the door behind him, she leaned against it. Her legs were shaking. Drake Dixon had given her a huge opportunity when he contracted with her for the clubhouse and luxury box meals before Gems games. There were any number of legitimate reasons he would be checking on her. Maybe.

Just because she couldn't think of one didn't mean anything.

"I'm bored." Tag's wheelchair blocked the entrance to the kitchen.

She'd shown up late morning and in a pissy mood. Slamming around his kitchen like she owned it. "Call Bluto back and do some more PT," she suggested.

"That's cruel."

"I'm the cook, not the entertainment."

"Who whizzed in your cereal this morning?"

"You don't want to know." Her mutter was so low Tag wondered if he was meant to hear it.

Containers filled with hard-boiled egg whites drenched in orange liquid covered every available flat surface. The entire penthouse reeked of sulfur.

"What are you doing?"

"I'm summoning demons to make you leave me alone," Red snapped.

"Ha. Ha. The Cooking Comedienne. We could get you a spot on the cable access channel. Why are you dying those eggs?"

"Deviled eggs for a Halloween party."

"I like deviled eggs." His mom made the best ones he'd ever had. Of course, the eggs she'd used were taken that morning right from the nests in the chicken coop. Nowadays, they'd be called organic or some such nonsense.

"These are for a party. I'll make you some tomorrow to snack on during the game."

"So what do you devil them with?"

Red stopped whatever she was doing with her big knife and stared at him. "Isn't there a Thursday-night football game for you to watch or something?"

"I hate football."

"No, you don't. You're a guy. You get off on violence." She returned to jabbing at green stuff on her cutting board.

"The game doesn't start for a couple of hours yet. And don't stereotype. It's unattractive."

"I thought we cleared this up already. I'm not trying to attract you."

"You're doing a lousy job."

A real lousy job. The more time he spent in her company, the more he liked her. And, pondering that, he was wondering just what they could do in a wheelchair. Or his bed. His right leg might be busted up and he might be doped to the hair follicles on his head, but last night's hard-on had been real enough. And it wasn't just a reaction to a woman's soft ass resting on his lap. He'd dreamed about her most of the night.

"I guess my knife-wielding persona isn't scaring you off. Pity. I'll be sure to wear a hag outfit tomorrow." Her tone was neutral. "Now go amuse yourself."

He didn't think an ugly costume would help. All he could think about was her naked with him inside her. Was she a natural redhead? He'd never slept with a real ginger before.

"I've been thinking," he said.

"Don't. Focus your energy on your leg."

"You're a laugh a minute. Anyway, since you'll be watching tomorrow night's game here, why don't you plan on spending the night?" That sounded innocent enough.

Again, she paused in her chopping or mincing or whatever the hell she was doing with that knife to stare at him.

"I'm just thinking about you."

"Thanks." She sounded as sincere as his offer had been.

"So what did you say the problem with your building was?"

"I didn't. And it's nothing for you to think about. If you're so bored, tell me about yourself. Unload."

She resumed her task.

"I will if you will," he replied. "Actually, you can look me up on the team website. My official bio is there. But yours isn't on your website."

"I'm just a cook. What you see is what you get."

Maybe she was brushing him off, but she'd given him an idea about what to do with himself.

October 28, World Series Game 3

Why were baseball games on so late on the East Coast? Skye stifled a yawn as she added horns and wickedly angled eyebrows to a dozen deviled eggs. The day had been a long one.

Tag had already been to the kitchen twice to remind her game three was starting at nine. "Seattle fans want to see their team play too."

Skye didn't care about Seattle fans. They weren't rooting for the Gems to win.

Then she realized she shouldn't be rooting for them to win either. She wanted the Gems to win the series at home. Where she'd be catering games six and seven. The bigger the down payment she could put on the stove, the less her monthly installments would be.

If she could make the balloon payment. But worrying wouldn't put the money in her bank account. Only a miracle could do that, and Skye hadn't given up on miracles yet. Hadn't the Gems made it to the Series? Hadn't the biggest shareholder of the team hired her to cater his Halloween bash? Hadn't her old stove finally given up the ghost so she was forced to purchase a new one?

Oh. Wait. That wasn't a miracle. That was bad timing. Unless she chose to look at it differently. And, just like her thinking during her could-have-been-miserable childhood, Skye chose to be positive.

"Come on, Red. They're singing the National Anthem." Tag was in the doorway of the kitchen in his wheelchair. She could have sworn Franz had already moved him to his recliner.

She said nothing as she sealed the tray of eggs with plastic wrap. Once the eggs had been refrigerated, Skye pulled out Tag's baseball-watching snack for the night.

"You go on ahead, and let Franz get you situated. I'll bring the food."

Tag was definitely acting weirder than usual.

She'd marinated bite-size chunks of chicken in a lemon garlic concoction and then skewered them on long wooden picks with chunks of mango, red bell peppers, and thick rings of sweet onion. Using Tag's marvelous stovetop grill, she'd cooked them to perfection and then chilled them. She'd roasted the almonds herself to ensure their oil and salt content. And what was a baseball game without popcorn in a helmet? It had taken some doing, but she had connections at the stadium. The only difference was her popcorn was air-popped and lightly misted with real butter.

She placed the food on the card table Franz had left next to Tag's recliner.

Tag didn't say anything as he munched his way through five innings. The score was tied. The last thing Skye wanted to do was try to stay awake for extra innings.

She almost wished she'd taken Tag up on his invitation to spend the night. She didn't need heat yet, but cold showers were getting tiresome.

The death of the stove had created a chain reaction.

But she wasn't going to mope.

"All right!" she exclaimed when a Seattle player got on first.

"What the hell?" Tag asked. "You're rooting for the guys in teal, not the guys in white."

"No, I'm rooting for Seattle."

"Not in my house."

"Fine." She stood up. "Do you want me to leave the food out for you, or shall I put it away before I leave?"

"You're not going anywhere until the game is over. That's the deal. Remember?" Tag sounded grumpy.

Skye sat back on the smooth leather. "Cranky."

The next Seattle batter advanced the runner. Skye punched the air with her fist but said nothing.

Tag glared at her. "The Gems pay you."

"Not unless they're home," Skye replied. She desperately needed them back in Columbia.

When Seattle scored the go-ahead run, Skye couldn't help but whoop.

"If Seattle wins this game, you have to pay a forfeit," Tag said.

Skye didn't like the gleam in his eyes. "Says who?"

"Your host and client. If the Gems don't lose too badly, you'll be safe. Because for every run they lose by, you have to forfeit an item of clothing."

Skye tried to suppress her laugh, but it escaped as a snort. "Strip baseball?"

"Just think. We can start a new trend. Bring in more fans."

"Who'd only get bored between hits."

"I don't know. I don't think seeing you without your shirt would bore me. Probably just the opposite." His lips curved into a smirk. "And that could be a problem, given the fact I can't do anything about, well, you know." He even waggled his eyebrows.

Skye didn't try to hide this laugh. "You are so full of it."

"I'd rather be filling you with it."

It took a moment for her muzzy brain to process his crude comment. "You're out of line."

"No more so than you rooting for my enemy."

So that's how he wanted to play it. "Haven't you ever heard the old saying, 'Don't bite the hand that feeds you'?"

"Who's feeding who? You're being paid by the Gems to cook food the Gems are paying for to feed me, a Gem, in my hour of need."

Guilt slammed her. She couldn't refute a single thing he said. Still, she attempted to excuse her perceived betrayal. "The fans deserve to see the Gems take it all at home."

"The fans deserve to see us sweep Seattle into Puget Sound. *I* deserve to see the Gems annihilate Seattle."

"Seattle isn't responsible for what happened to your leg."

"My leg is responsible for the Gems being in Seattle."

She bit her lip. She wasn't going to whine to Tag. His leg would heal. The bone would mend. And he had the entire off-season to recuperate. If she lost her building, she might as well be losing her business. Yeah, Skye's the Limit was her, not the address or even the stove, but without a place to ply her trade, she was nothing. She didn't have an off-season. She had clients who trusted her to create the food of their fantasies.

But none of that had anything to do with Tag Gentry. The Gems paid him massive amounts of money to squat behind home plate and paint his fingernails white. The Gems paid his health insurance. For all the rehab he was going to need. For Hans, Franz, and Bluto. All of that, above and beyond his obscene salary.

If she got hurt at work, she was sunk.

Tag was still a have-it-all, and she remained a have-not.

Seattle beat the Gems three to two. Skye stood, took off her clogs, and threw them at Tag's head. "Two for one."

"Hey! Good thing you've got a lousy arm. If one of those had hit me, I might have to rescind my invitation for you to spend the night here."

"I'm not spending the night here. I have my own place. Besides, my goldfish needs to be fed."

"You can't afford a goldfish." Tag scoffed. "You live over your catering business, and the power company shut off your gas."

Skye's head jerked up. "I beg your pardon?"

He smirked. "I've been looking you up on the Internet, Celeste. Who gave you that god-awful name? No wonder you call yourself Skye."

"At least you can't make obscene rhymes with it. Tucker." Her mouth was dry. What exactly was floating around about her?

His smirk widened. "I have a brother named Hunter. The cheerleaders in high school had this chant—"

"I don't want to hear it."

"They got real creative with my brother Cooper's name too."

"I'll bet they did. Good night. I'll see you in the morning."

"You need a loan to pay your gas bill?"

Skye squared her shoulders and headed for the foyer. "No. Thanks, though."

"I know. You *need* cold showers after hanging out with me."

A little too close to the truth. "Busted."

"We could fix that problem."

"You're the one with the problem. Good night."

October 29, World Series Game 4

The next morning, Red showed up at Tag's penthouse bleary-eyed, pissy, and loaded down with...stuff. Domestic kind of stuff.

He had to admit Red's version of baseball party food wasn't half-bad. Especially for healthy crap. But her temper? Good thing she couldn't throw for shit. Otherwise, he'd have been beaned by her shoes. Where did she get off abusing his hospitality? Rooting for the opposing team. Leaving out the leftovers so Franz had to deal with them. Refusing his offer of a place to stay.

Being pissy with him.

Besides, he wasn't in the mood for high-maintenance women. That was another thing that suited him about Terra Baldwin. She was so low maintenance, he didn't even think about her often. Mostly when he was bored or horny. Otherwise, women were a distraction he didn't need.

There were guys who could mix marriage with being on the road more than half the year but most couldn't. Fidelity in the face of groupies was a struggle. He indulged. Not often. Most of those women were unstable and a few were whack jobs. One of the relief pitchers had been stalked by a woman he'd fucked in Washington. It had gotten scary and ugly really fast.

Some of the guys had regular girlfriends in several of the National League cities. Even some of the married men. What was the point of being married if you were just going to crawl between any pair of female thighs whenever the urge struck?

Like it was striking with Red. The more time he spent in her company, the more he realized just how badly he wanted to get her naked.

Tag figured he wasn't cut out for marriage and family. Oh, his folks were still married, maybe even happily so. But Tag's father had been exhausted more often or not, working hard to feed his brood of children. Tag had never felt unloved, but he'd never felt like an individual either. Unless he was in trouble. That was the only time he had either parent's undivided attention.

Life on the farm hadn't been easy. Boring, yes. Simple. Not particularly. Easy? Never.

He'd known early on that baseball was going to be his way out. Baseball was suited to his temperament. Traveling all the time during the regular season. Having the money and the time in the off-season to seek new experiences. He'd been fined by the team more than once for reckless behavior, but bungee jumping off Bloukrans Bridge in South Africa had been worth the extra money. So had shark diving in Cape Town.

There was something about Celeste Schuyler that intrigued him the same way. Which made no sense. If anything, she was a nester. One of those women who wanted to feed everybody chicken soup and sew on their shirt buttons. He shouldn't be attracted, unless it was by her air of unattainability. And there was only one way to deal with that.

Get pissy back.

"I don't think the Gems should be paying you to feed me, when I'm paying the electric bill for your catering business." Tag's wheelchair was once more parked in his kitchen. He'd spent more time in that room since breaking his leg than he had in the six years he'd lived in the penthouse. His entire world had come down to pain and torture with Bluto and trying to rile Red. Who gave him plenty of ammo.

Take the food accumulating in his refrigerator. Like the deviled eggs. He loved deviled eggs, and there were trays of them, cleverly decorated for Halloween, under plastic wrap. He'd told her he liked deviled eggs. But there hadn't been any for his breakfast or his lunch.

And other shit was encroaching into his man cave. Midget pumpkins. Fake spider webs. A preponderance of orange and black *stuff*. Orange and black were not the Gems' team colors.

"What's this crap?" he asked.

"Halloween decorations." She was squeezing goop from a plastic bag onto cupcakes. Fancy swoops and swirls. More orange. She didn't look at him.

"Isn't Saturday the big night for Halloween parties? How are you going to cater a party and still watch the game with me?"

"When the Gems got into the Series, Mr. Dixon rescheduled from tonight until Halloween itself. And because of the scope of his party, I didn't book any others."

How convenient was it that Halloween happened to fall on a travel day? If the Gems didn't win the next two games in Seattle.

The he realized what she'd said.

"Mr. Dixon? As in Drake Dixon? As in the majority shareholder of the Gems?"

"The same." Red seemed awfully nonchalant.

Tag didn't like Drake Dixon. Just because he was a Gems shareholder didn't make the guy a decent human being. Tag didn't like the idea of Red working for Dixon either. She must have mentioned it at some point, but it hadn't sunk in. "Why isn't this crap at his house instead of mine?"

"I thought I would take everything over at once."

She added an orange flourish to an already overdecorated cupcake. And she still wouldn't look at him.

"So how did you get the job for Dixon?"

"I cater for the luxury boxes at the stadium, and Mr. Dixon liked what he tasted."

More likely he liked what he saw with Red. Dixon was worse than the horniest player when it came to women. Tag had heard plenty of rumors. Nasty stuff.

Dixon wasn't just a dog. He was a wealthy hound, and his kind of wealth could buy all sorts of things. Like silence.

Tag studied Red. She seemed unconcerned about Dixon's reputation. Maybe she was one of those women who didn't care about dark rumors and who liked to live dangerously. Maybe she wanted Dixon to try something with her. That would be one way to pay her gas bill.

That ugly thought didn't sit well. Tag didn't want to think of Red as the type of woman who'd sell herself so cheaply.

If she was going to put herself on the block, she ought to consider him. Maybe Tucker Alexander Gentry wasn't as wealthy as Drake Dixon, but his income as a player was somewhere between embarrassing and obscene. If Red wanted a fling with a rich bastard, why not with him instead of Dixon? Unless she wanted hush money.

He watched Red arrange the cupcakes on a platter and then snap a plastic cover over them.

He didn't like where his thoughts were going. Time to change the subject. "What's for dinner? Leftovers from last night?" The chicken on a stick had been pretty good.

"I don't get paid to feed you leftovers."

There. She was talking about money again.

He got that she was a working stiff, that he was just another job for her. Maybe he wasn't rich enough for her.

Even worse, maybe he was her plan B.

He turned his wheelchair around and headed for his office.

A little more digging around gave him a better picture of Red's situation. In addition to the gas cut-off, she had a balloon payment due on her mortgage. No wonder she was using his kitchen. She was desperate, not horny.

Tag had to admire her fortitude. The way she worked to honor her commitments. The whole balloon-payment thing sucked. No wonder she'd been rooting for Seattle last night. She really did need the Gems to play the last two games at home.

He called his agent. Marty Fiscoe's talent agency was full-service, so Tag knew Marty would get the financial branch working on purchasing Red's loan from the bank.

Better to purchase the mortgage than pay it off for her. She clearly had pride to go along with her gumption. Tag couldn't fault her for that. He could do her a little favor, and she'd never know. He figured if he held the loan instead of the bank, he could give her a little more leeway than she was getting from the institution.

"The mortgage isn't for sale," Marty told him several hours later.

"That's ridiculous," Tag replied as he tried to dislodge part of a lettuce leaf from between his back molars. Mortgages were always for sale. "Did you say it was for Tag Gentry?" He half expected his name to expedite the process. His name meant something in this city. Or it had the week before. Maybe not now that he was benched.

"Actually, it's already in the process of being sold to someone else. Why do you want that crappy old building anyway?"

Someone else? Who would want an abandoned restaurant in that part of Columbia? "I don't. I was just trying to do someone a favor."

"You're thinking with your dick," Marty replied. "Is the caterer really that good?"

It was one thing for Tag to have those thoughts. He didn't like hearing them from Marty.

Tag went with one version of the truth. "She's camped out here doing her cooking, including for a party she's catering for Drake Dixon."

Marty muttered something about sadistic sleazeball pedophiles. So *he'd* heard things too. "Why do you want to help someone involved with him?"

"So she doesn't have to be." Tag didn't need to think about his response. "I don't think she knows about him. She's just happy for the work."

He hated thinking what the cost of Dixon's interest in Red might be.

"You stay out of Dixon's business." Marty's voice was as flat and hard as a tombstone.

"I wasn't planning on getting into it," Tag replied. He knew how much power Dixon had over his career with the Gems. And Red was a big girl. She could handle herself.

Tag only wished his gut wasn't as knotted as one of the macramé plant holders his mom was so fond of making.

"Is there any way you can find out who's buying her mortgage?"

Skye worked on Halloween appetizers all afternoon. Dixon's menu consisted of hors d'oeuvres and a buffet of finger foods, which made advance prep easy. When Tag wasn't underfoot, questioning her every motive.

Her daily call to the bank to ask for a week-long grace period didn't go well. All she asked for was seven stinking days. She even tried dropping Drake Dixon's name, hoping to impress with the quality of the work she had on tap. As usual, the bank refused to negotiate.

She disconnected the call and hung her head.

When she looked up again, it was into Tag's gray gaze.

"Rough day?" he asked.

She curved her lips, even though smiling was the last thing she felt like doing. "Praying for inspiration for your supper tonight."

Not true. She'd already broiled a tenderloin and saved aside mixed greens from his luncheon salad.

"Don't let me keep you, then. I know you have to suck up to Drake Dixon."

For some reason, every time Tag mentioned Dixon, his voice took on a sneer.

Maybe he was jealous because Dixon had so much more money. It had been her experience that those who had always wanted more.

"So did you get yourself settled in?"

"What are you talking about?" Skye reached for her big chef's knife.

Tag didn't miss her action. His eyes narrowed. "The guest room. The one you're sleeping in tonight."

Now they were back to that. "I'm going home after the game. I don't want to displace Franz."

"I have more than one guest room." Now Tag sounded impatient. "And a couple of them have their own bathrooms. With hot water coming out of the showerheads."

Skye narrowed her eyes back at him. No fair luring her with the promise of a hot shower.

"This apartment isn't furnished," she said. "There probably aren't any beds in your guest rooms."

"Are looking for an invitation to my bed?" Tag snorted. "I have furniture. Where do you think my family stays when they come to visit?"

"A hotel?"

"Not my family."

As if she would know how families functioned.

The prospect of a hot shower convinced her he was right. She'd been there since early in the morning, and who knew when the final out would happen? And really, what could Tag Gentry do from his wheelchair?

Her cheeks heated as she recalled that moment on his lap. Maybe the wheelchair wasn't that much of a deterrent. Her small crush on Tag was growing, and her imagination took that moment and turned the wheelchair into something that could be managed. As long as the brakes were on.

Skye didn't flatter herself.

Because Tag hadn't reacted to *her*. Any female under the circumstances would have caused his erection. For all she knew, maybe Franz, Bluto, and Hans had to deal with his rampant sexuality.

A couple of hours later, they'd resumed their poses in front of his television.

"How about a kiss for luck?" he asked her during the playing of the National Anthem.

"The Gems do better when I ignore that question."

Tag was quiet for the rest of the evening. Skye had a sense he wasn't entirely focused on the game.

Maybe he was regretting his invitation. She hadn't brought a bag with her. Leaving after the game wouldn't be at all awkward. She closed her eyes for just a moment.

"High five!" Tag crowed.

Skye pried her eyes open. The game was over. She rubbed her finger along the corner of her mouth, hoping to catch any drool before it spotted the leather of the sofa. "Who won?"

"Would I want a high five if Seattle had won?"

"Don't be surly," Skye said. Every cell in her body felt logy.

"I'm not surly. What the hell is surly? You're supposed to watch baseball with me, not sleep in front of the TV."

"Cranky, then." Skye's jaw cracked as she yawned.

"Winning bores you?"

"I'm not bored. Just tired."

"Yeah. You snored through six innings."

"I don't snore."

"News flash. You snore like Homer Simpson."

The gleam in his steel-gray gaze could have meant anything from anger to teasing. His mood actually had to be good. Hadn't the Gems won?

Skye stood and stretched. Her spine popped in a good way. "Congrats on the win."

When she looked at Tag again, he was still watching her.

"What?" She rubbed the corners of her mouth again. His scrutiny made her uncomfortable.

"High five." He held up his arm, palm facing her. "You get to keep your clothes tonight."

"I don't play strip baseball." But she crossed to him and patted her hand against his.

His fingers closed around hers. He tugged her closer. She was still so sluggish from her nap that she drifted closer to him as if she were a balloon on a string.

"Want me to show you to your room?"

Skye pulled free from his grasp. "Nope. I'm going home tonight, but thanks for your generous offer." Maybe if she arrived early enough in the morning she could grab a hot shower. And maybe she'd pack a bag. Staying at his place would certainly save her commute time.

"Then a good-night kiss." Tag reached for her again.

"What's with you?" Skye took several steps back from him.

"Has a day ever gone by when I haven't asked you for a kiss when I saw you?"

"Okay. Now you've asked. Good night." She turned to leave.

"Wait."

She stopped. Braced herself. Turned to face him. "What?" He merely stared at her. "The next two days are going to be really difficult. I can't blow this party for Mr. Dixon. I'm exhausted. I need to get home."

"What do you know about Drake Dixon?"

The question surprised her. "He's wealthy. He's the majority shareholder of the Gems." She shrugged. "He gives a lot of parties and pays his caterers really well."

"That's it?"

"Yeah. Why?"

Tag hesitated, as if reluctant to share his thoughts.

Skye tapped her foot, counting off the seconds before he continued.

"He has a bit of a reputation," Tag finally said. "Not a good one."

"For what? Not paying his bills?" That was the only thing she cared about.

"For not treating women very well." Tag practically snapped the words. "And I don't want to see you getting sucked into his perverted games."

"Perverted?"

"I've heard the reason he pays so well is because a good portion of the remittance is hush money."

"I don't listen to gossip." Skye turned again to leave. It was sweet of Tag to try to warn her, but Dixon wouldn't try anything funny with the hired help. That was all she was.

"That's commendable, but I'm still worried about you."

She whirled to face him. "Why should you worry about me?"

He looked as if he were going to say something...profound and then shrugged. "I don't want to have to break in a new cook, and I'm pretty sure neither Hans nor Franz can do more than run the microwave."

"I'm here for the duration. But I need to go home."

"You need a cold shower after being with me?"

"Something like that."

"Are you sure you don't want a short-term loan to pay your gas bill?"

Skye blinked. "Where did you come up with that? I pay my bills."

"I was wondering what exactly kind of problems you were having with your building, so I did some research—"

"You had no right!" Fury turned her blood to boiling lava.

"You're using my facilities to earn your living. I have every right to know what I'm getting into." His jaw set in a stubborn line.

Crimson rage hazed her vision. "You didn't snoop deep enough. The power company turned off the gas in my building because my stove is so old the only way to stop the leaking was to shut off the gas."

He seemed surprised. "You need a cold shower now," he muttered.

Oh, if there were something nearby to toss at his stubborn thick head, she would have snatched it up and thrown. Her gaze went to the card table set up next to his recliner. His empty plate, fork, and knife were waiting to be cleared. Too bad his serrated table knives weren't sharp enough to do serious damage to his thick hide.

But to reach the implements, she'd have to stretch across Tag. And that would not only be foolish, it would be dangerous.

His quip about cold showers wasn't that far off mark. Her little crush was growing like a loaf of soda bread gone wild.

"What else did you learn with your spying?" She needed to keep him at a distance, and the best way was to pick a fight.

"You have a balloon payment due in three days. Which is why you want the Gems at home to win the Series. You get paid pretty well to feed the team. Do you think the bank will negotiate a new date with you?"

"I'm working on it. All I need are two days. It's not as if anyone else wants the building. I mean, yeah, it's worth more now than when I acquired it because I've done a lot of work on it, but it's still a rundown building in a rundown part of town."

Rundown was a nice way to describe the neighborhood.

And why was she spilling her guts to Tag?

She clamped her mouth shut and headed for the foyer, where her purse hung in the coat closet.

CONFLICT TORE AT Tag's gut. "Red. Wait." Everything about her situation bothered him. Maybe because Dixon was involved.

She kept walking away.

He pounded on the arms of his recliner. "Damn it, Red!" he shouted as she disappeared from view. "Get back here, and clean up after my meal. It's not Franz's job."

He cursed himself for using such a lame excuse.

She was short-circuiting his brain. That and being stuck in the damned recliner until Franz or Hans moved him to his wheelchair. If he wanted to report to spring training in February, he had to stay in the chair instead of attempting to go after her.

"Where is your professional pride?" he called after her. The sound of the closet doors sliding open, the metallic clang of coat hangers knocking together, the doors closing with a bang. But the front door of his apartment didn't open. She hadn't left the premises yet.

"Or have you figured out pride won't save you?"

Red reappeared in the door. It might have been the lousy light in his living room, but she seemed pale. "Says the man who messed up his leg getting his team to the World Series and is now pouting because he's not there playing."

"That's not pride. That's pissed off."

Her pocketbook was draped across her body. She came closer to him. Her movements were jerky and hesitant. She was usually so much more graceful, especially in the kitchen.

"The bank doesn't own your mortgage." Why was he telling her this? "I tried to buy it myself."

She flinched as if he'd punched her.

"They're in the process of selling to someone else. They don't have to tell you until it's a done deal."

"To whom? Why?"

"I don't know. And I'll bet they're not being very cooperative with you."

"They're not. But I'm calling them every day. I'll have all the money by the third of the month. If I bug them enough, maybe they'll agree to a few days just to make me stop."

"If the Gems play two more games at home."

She nodded. "And there's Drake Dixon's party, and a political event on the eighth. All of them are going to pay really well."

Dixon's gig had to have been scaled back after he'd moved it from Saturday to Monday.

He honestly didn't know where his next words came from. "You want a fifteen-day loan?" Why was he sticking his nose in her business? He didn't lend money to people.

She opened her mouth, and he noticed, not for the first time, how full and plump her lips were. Lips that had been so incredibly soft beneath his own.

"I can't take your money."

Her refusal surprised him.

"It's a loan. For fifteen days."

She shook her head. "It's not that I don't appreciate your offer, but Skye's the Limit is my business. I have to do this on my own."

"All I'm offering is another loan. And you can keep your clothes on."

Her smile was crooked. "Thank you, but I won't be beholden to anyone. Not even the hometown hero."

If she'd looked for a more sensitive spot to thrust her refusal, she couldn't have found one. "If I'd bought your loan, you wouldn't know it until thirty days after the fact. But the bank is retaining the servicing rights. Someone is going to a lot of trouble to hide the transaction from you."

She swallowed hard, muscles in the pale column of her throat working. "What do you mean?"

"You'll still be dealing with the bank that handled your first mortgage. And the public records will still indicate the bank holds the loan and is the contact. Have you received any notices from the bank or anyone else?"

"I don't think so."

"Well, I don't like it."

"It's not your business."

"It became my business when you moved in here with your cake pans and carving knives." Besides, he was the only one who could take advantage of Red. "I'm having someone dig a little deeper."

"Why?"

"Because I don't trust people who want to conduct business in secret, and that's what seems to be what is happening with your mortgage. Maybe your stove was sabotaged too."

"Oh, if only." Her eyelids drooped. "Then I could collect insurance. But that's not the case. I think the stove is older than the building. It just...gave up the ghost."

"What are you planning to do about that?"

"Not that it's any of your concern, but once I pay off the mortgage, I plan to take out another loan and buy the stove of my dreams."

Tag snorted. "You dream about stoves?"

"And kitchens. I've dreamed of my own kitchen my whole life."

Tag could understand the power of a dream. Wasn't he stuck in his recliner because of his determination to see the fulfillment of his own dream?

And there was something definitely wrong with the way the bank was handling her mortgage.

Red yawned again.

"That does it. You're not driving home tonight." He didn't understand why he felt so protective of Red. He admired her. She didn't whine. She simply did her job. Another woman might have hit him up for money—outright, not merely a loan. Instead, Red simply moved into his kitchen, which he wasn't using, and carried on.

He picked up his cell phone and punched in Franz's number. "I'm ready to go to bed." It was a bit embarrassing for him to have to depend on Franz, especially in front of a woman, but it couldn't be helped. "And I need you to show Red to the guest room across the hall from your room."

"I'm not spending the night with you, not even in a separate room with multiple locks on the door."

Tag's self-control was the only reason he didn't roll his eyes.

"Confiscate her keys," he told Franz. "She's too tired to drive."

October 30, World Series Game 5

Skye woke up with a crick in her neck. She cracked open one eye, feeling muzzy and disoriented. It took a moment before she realized she'd fallen asleep on one of Tag Gentry's burgundy leather sofas. Again.

The last thing she remembered about the previous evening was clearing away Tag's dinner dishes and arguing with him about her gas bill and whether or not she was spending the night. Oh, and Franz stealing her car keys. Looked like Tag had won.

She was still in the same jeans and three-quarter-sleeved T-shirt she'd worn the previous day. Ick. She yawned and stretched. Judging by the pinkish light coming through the terrace doors, it was just after dawn. She had time to run home and grab a shower before she hit the market for fresh produce.

No point showering unless she had clean underwear. Which she didn't.

Franz had left her keys on the kitchen counter.

It was a good thing she hadn't showered, because Drake Dixon was waiting in the alley outside Skye's the Limit. She nearly wet herself when she saw him.

"Skye. I've been worried. I tried stopping by yesterday, but you weren't around. The building looks deserted."

"I've been around," she said. She wondered if she should be nervous after the things Tag had hinted at. She'd never had a client so in her face before. "Getting things ready for your party tomorrow night. I think you're going to be really pleased. How did you find my building?"

"I'm sure I will be more than pleased." He seemed to ignore her question. "Do you have your costume yet?"

Costume? "I didn't realize you expected me to dress up. I mean, I'll be in the kitchen, keeping the food coming. My part-time server will be in her tux. We're not guests, Mr. Dixon, and don't expect to be treated as such."

"Oh, come on, Skye. You're part of the Gems family." He brushed the top of her shoulder as she unlocked the door.

She suppressed a shudder at his touch. "Congrats on last night's win. Is there something in particular you need?" *That you couldn't call me about?*

"No, just doing a follow-up before tomorrow night." His tone was unctuous. Or had Tag influenced her reaction?

And Dixon still hadn't answered her question about how he knew where her business was located.

"Everything is under control. I do need to head out to the market in a few minutes for my produce."

He smiled. "And here I am, keeping you from your work."

Another light caress, this one on her arm. Was she supposed to deny that he was in the way? She returned his smile. "I'll see you tomorrow night."

Dixon hesitated and then seemed to take the hint. He climbed into his luxury SUV.

Skye locked the door behind her, leaned against it, and inhaled deeply. What in the world had that been about?

Three hours later, she stood in the lobby of Tag's building with two rolling coolers and her overnight bag, waiting for the leisurely elevator. When the elevator doors slid open, Franz stepped out.

"There you are." He looked tired. "The boss is in a tizzy. You vanished on him."

"I went home. Then to the market." Not that she owed anyone—especially not Tag—an explanation. She glanced at her watch. She was arriving at the same time she'd shown up the previous morning.

Franz yawned. Hugely. "See you tonight."

The apartment was silent when she opened the door. She dropped her overnight bag in the foyer closet. Spending the night in Tag's apartment made sense. She needed to watch game five with him to pay rent on the kitchen. And his TV was bigger than hers, making it easier to study the players. They were tired. The change in time zone was messing with their metabolisms and adding to their stress. Plus she'd get a jumpstart on the last-minute preparations for Dixon.

She began layering thawed shrimp in a clear glass bowl while she roasted a red bell pepper in the center of one of the burners. The kitchen started taking on the aroma of charred pepper skin.

Tag wheeled in when she was cutting the pepper into long, thin strips.

"Where were you?" he asked.

She didn't like his tone. "I went home to change my clothes. Then to the market. I've got a busy day ahead of me." She tucked a strip of pepper around several of the shrimp. She'd already decided not to tell him about Dixon's visit. Either of them.

"I thought you were staying here last night." He sounded as petulant as a child.

"I didn't have a choice after Franz confiscated my keys. At your command." Skye did her best to remain serene. She'd never built a brain from shrimp before and wanted to concentrate on the process. Everything for the Dixon party had to be perfect. "And I'll stay tonight too. I even brought a change of clothes for tomorrow. Now you have to leave me alone. I need to finish this brain. Then work on the green fingers, bloody eyeballs, gutsy hummus, and a bunch of other things." People didn't understand how long it took to make everything look just right. Presentation was just as important as flavor.

"For Dixon." Now Tag was growling.

"For *Mr.* Dixon. He's paying the bills." Skye put the gelatin and chicken broth mixture on the stove and turned on the burner. Her spoon clanged against the side of the pan. Maybe too vigorously. Dixon's visit had shaken her, but she couldn't let Tag know.

"I'll lend you the money you'll make from his party, plus whatever else you need to make your mortgage payment."

"We've already had this conversation."

"Damn it. I don't want you working for him."

"I already work for him." Hadn't he just reminded her? "Every home game, I feed the team, I cater to the luxury suites, and I'm cooking for you while you're healing."

Tag didn't say anything as she whisked the rest of the ingredients into the broth-gelatin base. Lemon, tomato paste, honey, garlic, and ginger. Oh, this was going to be fabulous.

"Don't worry. I won't forget to feed you before the party."

"I have every faith in you. It's Dixon I don't trust."

"If I'd known you'd carry on like this, I never would have mentioned whose party I was catering." She poured the mixture over the shrimp and red pepper strips. The already-pink shrimp took on an even rosier hue.

"What is that supposed to be?" Tag stared at the masterpiece.

"A brain. I'll carve another one out of watermelon tomorrow."

"I wish you'd use the one in your skull. Dixon doesn't deserve all the work you're putting into this party."

"He's paying for it." Why did she have to keep reminding Tag that catering was how she earned her living?

Tag snorted his opinion and wheeled out of her way.

Good. She wanted to perch on the stool and start prepping the radishes for the eyeball tray. She'd been looking forward to assembling the eyeball tray since she'd booked the event.

As long as she kept busy, she couldn't dwell on Dixon.

HOW COULD ONE woman be so stubborn? Tag wheeled himself to his office and slammed the door. He had an e-mail from the private investigator Marty had hired to look into Red's mortgage situation. The company purchasing her loan was privately held, but Marty's investigator was good. Tag read through the web of false fronts.

Drake Dixon was buying the mortgage on Celeste Schuyler's property.

Vivid purple lights exploded in Tag's brain.

"Hans!" he bellowed.

When the day nurse opened the door, Tag narrowed his eyes. "We have things to do."

The eyeball tray was a masterpiece. The radish and pimento-stuffed green olive rendition ringed the edge of the platter. The center was filled with a Caprese version, complete with fragrant basil leaves and moist, fresh mozzarella. She'd already made another plate with deviled eggs, but they weren't nearly as spectacular as the veggie-based eyeballs.

If Skye wasn't so pleased with the outcome, she might have been more sensitive to Tag's cranky mood. He picked at his lunch and wasn't much better with his dinner, even though she'd once again caved to his love of steak.

She experimented with organic beef hotdogs wrapped in whole-grain pastry to mimic mummies for his game-time snack. She thought he might be in a better mood by the time nine o'clock rolled around, but he wasn't. He communicated in growls and snarls but insisted she stay in the room while the game was on. He didn't even ask her for a kiss.

When the cameras showed the owner of the Seattle team in his luxury box, Skye wondered why Dixon hadn't followed the Gems to the West Coast. He was the majority shareholder, and this was the World Series. But then, what did she understand about the day-to-day life of big businessmen? She was barely keeping herself afloat.

When the Gems lost and her sigh of relief filled the emptiness between them, he glared at her.

"I suppose you're happy."

"I haven't made any secret about wanting the Gems at home and why."

"Are you spending the night here?"

"Unless you want me to leave." She hoped he didn't. She was worn out. Her struggling to stay awake for the game should have counted as several hours of exercise. But she wasn't going to stay where she wasn't wanted.

And she wasn't sure she wanted to go to her apartment over the restaurant. Not with Dixon popping by. She didn't need to believe Tag to listen to her own instincts.

She got up to clear away Tag's dirty plates. He caught her wrist, wrapping his warm fingers tightly around the slender bones.

"What?" she asked.

His arm hooked around her waist. He tugged her into his lap again. Odd how she didn't mind it much when Tag manhandled her, but a casual touch from Drake Dixon twisted her stomach. Tag's huge hands rested on her ribs, outside her shirt but just under her bra band.

"What?" she asked again.

"I've grown fond of you," Tag said. The heat from his palms penetrated the cotton of her T-shirt.

She bit her lip to keep from saying anything. Her crush wasn't so little anymore, even if Tag was a moody jerk half of the time.

"I would hate like hell to see you get hurt by Dixon."

"I'm a big girl. I can take care of myself." What could Dixon do with penthouse full of guests? Besides, she planned to be in the kitchen all night.

Tag was becoming aroused. She shouldn't be sitting on his lap. "Do you want me to get up?"

His gray gaze seeped into her very pores, like smoke infiltrating every crevice. "What do you think?"

"You must be uncomfortable."

He ran a thumb down the side of her breast. Her nipple perked up as if to say, *Hey! Over here!*

"I've been more comfortable," he admitted. His thumb made a return trip. "You know, being in this wheelchair kind of limits my activities." He shifted his thighs, which increased the pressure of his erection against her bottom.

She needed to get off his lap. Needed to remind herself that he was bored, and she was convenient. Instead, she tilted her head to look Tag in the eye.

He must have thought the gesture was an invitation to kiss her.

This time, he started out slow, his lips barely brushing hers. The contact was like cold butter in a hot skillet, melting straight down to where Tag was letting her know he was aroused. Her little crush expanded and spread like a puddle. He ran his thumb up her throat, scarcely making contact with her sensitive skin. The bottom of her chin had never felt so fragile or so vulnerable.

When he clamped her jaw as he deepened the kiss, she let her entire body relax against his. The collapse wasn't conscious, but resting against Tag's broad chest was so right. His tongue, sweeping her mouth, was the definition of right. She'd thought she was better than a fan girl. She thought she was above being a jock's plaything. Tag's mouth on hers proved both assumptions to be lies.

Skye wasn't passive. If this thing between them was going to happen, she wanted to be more than a recipient. He wasn't the only one who could...touch.

The scruff on his unshaven face bristled against her fingers but softened under her palm. His skin was warm. Much warmer than hers.

She knew she shouldn't be kissing him. He was her customer. Catering did not include sexual favors. This was Tag Gentry, the ballplayer who used the past tense of his own name when referring to the women with whom he'd had sex. He'd been asking for her kisses since April but couldn't be bothered to use her chosen name.

So what did that make her, sitting on his lap, returning his kiss, reveling in how perfectly her breast fit in the palm of his strong catcher's hand? Except he had brushed ever so slightly against the secret girl she'd once been by allowing her to take care of him and was excavating the debris around the woman she longed to become, independent and strong.

He slid his hand under her T-shirt and into her bra and pinched her nipple. Rubbed his erection harder against her bottom. He rested his forehead against hers.

"We need to figure out how to do this." His whisper was harsh.

Not that she hadn't wondered once or twice how sex in a wheelchair would work. Easier when he was the one confined, that was for sure.

"Call Franz," she said. Her own voice wasn't much steadier than his.

"I'm not sharing. At least, not tonight."

Her laugh was shaky too. "Me either. But call him. Then call me when you're ready."

"I'm already ready."

She reached between them. Cupped his penis and squeezed ever so gently. Tag's breath hitched. "I noticed."

She didn't want to embarrass him by spelling out everything, but he was a guy with no blood left in his brain. "Call me when you're in bed," she repeated.

"Phone sex isn't going to cut it for me."

"Me either." She traced his bottom lip with her forefinger until his tongue snaked out and captured it. He gently sucked it into his mouth. The throbbing between her legs syncopated with the suction. He teased her with the acrobatics of his tongue, igniting her imagination of what that tongue could do to other parts of her body.

She had to leave him now or embarrass herself and possibly Franz, who could come to check on Tag at any moment.

"Call me." Her legs shook as she fled to the foyer, where she'd stashed her overnight bag in the coat closet.

She'd never been around when Hans, Franz, or even Bluto helped Tag from recliner to wheelchair to bed to whatever they did with him. Nor did she want to witness the process now. So she took her bag into the kitchen to wait.

Tag was intensely masculine and very physical. Being so dependent on others had to infuriate him, no matter how temporary the situation was.

"Hey, Red!" Tag called out a few minutes later. "Where are you? Let us show you to your room.

So she rejoined Franz and Tag in the living room and then trailed the wheelchair as Tag rolled down a hallway she'd never noticed. Franz opened one of the doors.

"My room," Tag said. "You're across the hall from Franz, who's next door."

"I didn't know night nurses slept," was all she could think of to say.

"I watch infomercials on TV," Franz muttered.

"Don't worry about it," Tag said at the same time. "The way you snore, you'll keep us all up all night."

Tag didn't engage in his usual banter with Franz as the nurse helped him get ready for bed. Nor did he try to explain away the half-mast boner he sported. Franz was a professional. He knew better than to comment on anything he saw in a client's home. Maybe someday, Tag would get used to needing help with everything, including the bathroom, but he didn't think it would happen in this lifetime.

In a blink, Tag flashed forward to the future. After baseball. After youth. After mobility. This, he thought as Franz steadied him so he could do his business, was a glimpse into the future.

He hated it. He would rather be dead than useless or helpless.

He told Franz he was going to sleep in the raw that night, something Franz tried to discourage.

"What if there's a fire? We won't have time to try to pull your shorts on over your cast before we need to evacuate."

"I'll drape a sheet over my lap."

After Franz left him, Tag reconsidered calling Red. He wasn't in the mood. Thinking about the future, facing the possibilities, was depressing as hell. What if this injury really had destroyed his career? What would he do if he couldn't play baseball? Oh, he knew there were thousands of answers out there. The most obvious were coaching or broadcasting. But the world was filled with former players, whereas the number of coaching, scouting, and broadcasting jobs were finite. And pathetic. Washed-up athletes unable to let go.

He was going to die of boredom. He could see his obit now: *Tucker Alexander Gentry, Columbia Gems catcher who sacrificed his leg so his team could win the World Series, passed away of boredom because he could no longer do anything.* Beyond baseball, he was worthless.

Oh, he had money. That's wasn't his concern. But not being able to *do*. That scared the piss out of him. Sometimes, since his injury, he couldn't sleep at night for wondering.

But tonight he wasn't going to wallow. Tonight, he was going to get laid.

He picked up his phone and began scrolling through his contacts. Maybe sleeping with the help wasn't such a good idea, but at least he'd feel alive. Better than the alternative. Besides, Red had become so much more than merely the woman who cooked for him. He liked her. She made him laugh. She didn't let him feel too sorry for himself, and she respected his priorities. She had honor.

Tag didn't usually think of women in terms of honor, but Red was the embodiment of honor. That was the biggest reason he was so furious about all her hard work on the Halloween party for Drake Dixon, who was worse than dishonor. Dixon used women like Red Schuyler and then tossed them in a gutter like so much garbage.

Tag hated to think of Red being abused and abased like that. Especially since she didn't see it coming.

He swiped her name in his contacts.

"Hey there." Her voice was low. Sultry.

"Having second thoughts?" he asked. He had been. He wanted to be honest with Red.

"A few. You?"

"Some. I mean, you know that if we follow through, it's just a hookup."

"I know."

"I like you and all, but I'm not a settling-down kind of guy." He didn't mention Terra. He barely gave his alleged significant other a thought.

Red cleared her throat. "I was thinking more along the lines of friends with benefits."

"Yeah. Friends." He liked that. He wanted to be friends with Red. Pals. Sit around and watch baseball together. Get naked with her. "Why don't you come on over, and let's see what we can figure out. Knock twice. Then let yourself in."

SKYE SLIPPED OFF her sleep shirt and pulled on her robe. She swallowed hard as she wrapped her fingers around the doorknob. Going to Tag's room was wrong on so many levels. First of all, it wasn't very professional. She'd avoided the temptation of flirting with baseball players all season. Secondly, she had to keep feeding him until he was able to get out and about. If things were dreadfully dreadful between them, that could prove to be a problem.

And now that she'd gotten to know him better, that little crush had grown to full-size. Her heart wanted more than friendship. Maybe the sex would be awful. That would be good, because it might cure her of her obsession with Tag.

Who went to a man's bed praying for bad sex?

Celeste Schuyler.

She had to get him out of her system. Their professional relationship was temporary. Okay, maybe she'd see him if the Gems renewed her contract for the following season. Maybe. From what she'd learned about his kind of injury, he might be out all of next season. So whatever happened tonight wouldn't matter in the long run.

Skye rapped on the door and then turned the knob.

Tag was in his bed, which looked as big as a baseball diamond. One lamp on the far side cast an oval of muted light which leeched the color from the carpet, the bedding, and the walls.

Heat swelled from her toes, oozing upward in defiance of gravity, until her cheeks burned.

"Come over here, Red." Tag patted the mattress.

She crossed the room, her feet unaware of the acrobatics in her stomach.

"Whatcha got on under that robe?" His eyes gleamed silver instead of their usual gray.

Skye pulled out the strip of condoms she'd tucked in her robe pocket and tossed them on the bed. Just so they would be on the same page.

Tag nodded. "I guess we're not playing games."

"No games. I thought we'd already determined that."

"Then take off the robe and get into bed."

The faux satin fabric shimmered in the dim light as Skye let the robe slip from her shoulders. The fabric flowed down her body like liquid until it puddled around her ankles. Faking a confidence utterly foreign to her, she raised one leg to kneel on the mattress.

Tag grasped her arms and pulled her next to him. "You're going to have to do most of the work here," he said. He tossed aside the sheet.

Skye's breath caught in her chest. He was beautiful. Worthy of a statue in his honor. She already knew he had broad shoulders and defined biceps, but his bare chest was a revelation. Muscled, but not overly so. A wedge of dark, silky-looking hair hid his nipples, then drew a trail down the prerequisite six-pack to his navel. But his innie belly button isn't what captured her attention.

Tag was big but not huge. She wouldn't have to worry about accommodating him. Sex was so much nicer when it didn't hurt.

Except she didn't want sex to be nice. Not with Tag. Because nice would be her undoing.

He reached for her breast. "I wondered what color your nipples were. Pretty. And you're a natural redhead."

She didn't know about pretty, but she knew they were as tight as radish roses before an ice-water bath.

"Come closer." His voice was husky. "I want to suck on you."

When his hot mouth closed over the tip of her breast, she flinched and then relaxed. He switched nipples but kept the other one company with surprisingly clever fingers.

She ached. She felt as if the past week had been foreplay. She stretched her palms over his pecs. His skin was hot. His chest hair was soft under her fingers. His heartbeat was steady and strong. Closing her eyes, she inhaled deeply. She wanted to imprint this moment on her memory for all time. He smelled of soap with a hint of perspiration—not dirty sweat but manly perspiration, which was a lot more honest than manly colognes.

She was going to have to take charge of what was going to happen. Tag's cast meant he was on his back and not mobile enough to initiate any change of...venue. For the first time in her life, she wished she was more experienced at this sort of thing. Seduction wasn't anywhere on her résumé. Not that she was a prude, a virgin, or anything like that. She just wasn't...adept with her sexuality. It was time to take matters into her own hands. Or at least Tag. Into her hands, that was.

Using her forefinger, she traced the path of his body hair down his chest and abdomen. When she got to his navel, the tip of his erection nudged the underside of her hand. A drop of wetness smeared onto her skin. His breath whistled sharply as she closed her palm around him. His penis was even hotter than his chest, and she wondered if it would leave scald marks on her flesh.

Her nipple slipped from Tag's mouth. His eyes were closed. "Red."

She tightened her grip and pumped once. "Skye."

"Red Skye tonight."

That would have to do.

Condom. But Tag had anticipated her thought and took care of sheathing his penis. Which was good. She would have fumbled and made a muck of it.

She swung her leg over his belly.

"Are you ready?" he asked.

She'd been ready for days but wasn't about to puff up his ego any more than it was already inflated. His reconnaissance discovered exactly how ready she was. A couple of his fingers explored further and deepened her need to take him inside her body.

Skye reached between their bodies. She grasped Tag's erection and held it steady as she positioned herself to sink onto him. He changed the focus of his fingers, concentrating on her clit instead of her vagina. The whimper clinging to her throat would stay there.

The man knew what he was doing.

His gasp as she began to lower herself onto him drowned out any other sound she might have made. She wanted to take him slowly, but her need for him roared to life and refused to budge.

Tag grasped her hips, as if he were trying to steady and direct the rhythm. But with one leg in a cast, his puny effort was easy to override. And ride over. She was in control. For once in her life, she was actually calling the shots, and she reveled in the sensation.

"Slow down," Tag groaned. His eyes remained shut, but his mouth was open with his heavy breathing. His nose was slightly wrinkled, as if he didn't know whether to smile or weep with pleasure.

She'd never seen that particular expression on anyone's face. Something else for her to remember.

"I'm not going to last."

"Then you'd better help me catch up, Mr. Catcher Man."

He opened his eyes, which now resembled tarnished silver. "That sounds like a challenge."

His gaze never flickered from hers as he removed one hand from her hip to burrow through her labia until he located her clit "Like this?"

Oh yeah. She nodded. Her eyelids drifted toward her cheeks. She thought she would anticipate her climax, but when orgasm came—when she came—it startled her. She sank onto Tag as far as she could. Her thighs, already stressed from the unaccustomed exercise, quivered from the intensity jolting through her. Her breathing wavered too.

If she'd had the energy, she would have climbed off him and curled against him to sleep. Instead, she collapsed against his chest. Her eyelids collapsed too.

"Oh, no you don't," Tag said, as he roused her. "It's my turn."

TAG WISHED HE could roll her over, crawl on top of her, and pound into her. And that, he promised himself, would be one of the first things he did when the cursed cast came off. In the meantime, he had to make do. All his control had gone into holding back until Red came.

Her climax was an experience to behold. Glorious was the word that came to mind. Her back arched, her breasts thrusting out. Her bright pink nipples were hard and tight—as tight as her pussy around his cock. Her eyes were closed. Red curls cascaded down her slender back. She was a vision. Her parted lips—those so soft lips—made him think of other things. Like blowjobs. Maybe later.

First he needed to finish fucking her.

He tried to curl upward to pull one of those nipples into his mouth, but without being able to brace his right leg, the task was impossible. So he did the only thing he could figure out to do and grabbed her ass. Got a firm grip on the soft globes. Red was pliant now. Flexible. Not fighting with him for control.

He lifted her. Brought her down. Repeated the sequence. Quickly. Found his rhythm. No finesse. No style. Just fucking to get off. It didn't take long. He'd been horny for Red for days. His orgasm seemed to last for hours, nearly blowing off the top of his skull.

When he finally released her hips, she collapsed to his side.

"Was that beneficial?" she asked.

OCTOBER 31, HALLOWEEN

The day started out so badly, Skye figured things could only get better.

She'd meant to crawl out of Tag's bed and sleep in the guest room to which she'd been shown. Instead, she fell asleep next to Tag, her head pillowed by his chest.

He was warm, and since the air-conditioning had been set to meat locker, she snuggled close. And stayed there until Tag woke her.

"You have to go back to your room before Franz comes in to help me to the bathroom." His voice was a low rumble against her ear. "And don't forget to take the used condom with you."

Right. He certainly couldn't dispose of it.

But was he protecting her reputation or his?

She would have been fine, except she ran into Franz in the hall. Oops. Not that he would say anything. Aloud. But looks spoke, and Skye didn't like what she heard.

The hot shower, bliss after days of cold ones, was about the only thing that went right. She still had the asparagus fingers and mummy meatballs to prepare, but she needed to do those at Dixon's apartment. Everything else was ready for transport. If she'd been at her own place, loading her van would be easy. Tag's twentieth-story penthouse made the trip from the refrigerators to the van a lot longer.

Tag. After his rough, early morning dismissal of her, he wasn't to be found. She tried to convince herself it was morning as usual at his place: the changing of the nursing staff, Bluto's arrival for Pain and Torture, and Hans assisting Tag with his shower and other personal needs. The atmosphere only felt different because of her second thoughts. Her guilt. Her worry that sex hadn't been at all mediocre for her despite being out of her comfort zone.

She knew Tag wasn't in top form—top anything. And she wasn't a top performer by choice. And the sex had still been better than okay. Maybe better than good. Maybe good enough that she wanted more, and that was dangerous.

But she couldn't dwell on Tag and her no-longer-little crush. Drake Dixon's party needed 100 percent of her attention. He was going to get what he paid for.

Then Skye's part-time employee called. Sick. Barely able to croak out her sorrow for letting Skye down on the biggest night of her career.

Tag found Red in the kitchen with her face in her hands. Her knuckles were white from pressing against her forehead.

"What's up, Red?"

Her hands dropped. Traces of wetness streaked her cheeks. "My server just called in sick. Where am I going to find someone to work for me tonight?" She squared her shoulders. "I guess I'll have to cook and serve."

"You've been cooking for days," Tag reminded her. "What more can you possibly do?"

"Things." She waved her hands toward the refrigerators.

Maybe she wasn't crying about the sick employee. Maybe she was crying because of him. Because of what had happened last night or that morning. He'd been brusque with her. He needed distance between them. Waking up with her draped across him had shocked him. He hadn't slept so well since his injury. No matter how hard he tried to convince himself it was the fucking that finally relaxed him, his conscience kept whispering it was Red, not sex.

Bluto's brutal paces had knocked some perspective into him. It was up to Tag to keep his friendship with Red on a light level. Females always wanted deeper, no matter what they said.

"Gina usually wears a tuxedo. It's very classy," Red mumbled.

"I'll help you." Tag hadn't meant to blurt the offer, but there it was.

"How?" She gestured toward his wheelchair.

He already had that part figured out. And it would work better than his original plan. "You leave that up to me."

"Change of plan, Hans," Tag said as he wheeled himself to his desk.

"Josh," Hans replied. "My name is Josh."

"Do you know if the supplies I ordered arrived yet?"

"I'm your nurse, not your flunky."

Tag glared at Hans while his computer booted up. "Don't be difficult. That's my role. I've decided against the shark cage. I want to do another costume."

"As I told you yesterday, I don't make Halloween costumes."

"There will be a bonus in it for you." Tag had run out of time to negotiate. He was going to Drake Dixon's party, even if he had to crash it. Which had been his plan right up until Red told him her server was sick. Now he had a legitimate reason to be there.

The Internet was a beautiful place and was populated by people who had way too much time on their hands. Like him. He'd typed in "Wheelchair Halloween Costumes" and watched the pictures fill the screen. Yesterday, he'd settled on a shark cage that looked fairly simple to assemble. After all, Dixon had fined him for shark diving just last winter.

But Tag had seen another costume, one that would not only assist him in helping Red serve but would also allow Franz to accompany him. Just in case. According to the website, he'd need only three things. The instructions for making it sounded simple. He already had one of the items. The other two were common and could probably be purchased at the pharmacy down the block from his building. Which, if he recalled correctly, delivered.

He pulled his phone from his pocket.

Drake Dixon was creeping Skye out. Big time. She might have only recently started Skye's the Limit, but she'd catered in a lot of people's homes before, kind of under the table. No one had ever...lurked the way Dixon was.

Or maybe Tag's warning had put icky thoughts in her head.

The first floor of Dixon's mansion has been tricked out in the most ghoulish display she'd ever seen. There was nothing campy or fantastical about the Halloween decorations. Maybe that was contributing to her discomfort. Because she wasn't comfortable. Even when Dixon wasn't in the room with her, she felt as if someone were watching her. Not just the heads in the jars or the leering skulls. Something alive. Breathing.

She ignored the hair on her nape standing at attention and the quivering in her stomach. This party was her big break. She was going to wow millionaires with her food. From the brains made from shrimp to the mummy meatballs and trays of fingers and eyeballs, she'd done her best. It *had* to be good enough.

"Where's your costume?" Dixon asked. While he technically didn't have her pinned down, there wasn't any way to walk away from him.

"I'm wearing it," she replied. She was in her chef whites.

He tsked.

Skye hadn't realized people actually did that, but Dixon was proof.

"There's no anonymity in that costume. No mystery. Intrigue."

"I hope your guests will be intrigued by the refreshments," Skye replied.

He smirked. There was no other way to describe his expression. "Your naïveté is intriguing. I suppose that will have to do."

"I don't recall sending you an invitation," Dixon said after he opened his front door and discovered Tag.

Bad luck there. Who'd have thought Dixon wouldn't have a servant to admit guests into his house?

"I'm bored, and I heard you were having a costume party. Since my catcher's mask is at the stadium, I had to come up with a different costume. Like it?" He gestured to the decked-in-red-and-white-checkered-linen table in front of him. The most difficult part of becoming a restaurant table was securing the table to the footrests of his wheelchair while still accommodating his broken leg. Everything else—a vase holding tiny skulls on stems and a basket for napkins—was anchored to the table with hook and loop fasteners.

Tag figured Red could put the foods she wanted passed around on the table, and he would mingle.

"Cute," Dixon replied. "But you weren't invited."

"Sure I was," Tag replied. "I'm the caterer's plus one."

"The caterer is working."

That was good news.

"And I'm here to help her serve. The woman who usually helps caught the flu. I felt bad for Red. She's been working really hard on this party." Tag figured truth was the best way to go in this situation. "She's expecting me."

"The service entrance is around back." Dixon started to close the door.

"And not wheelchair accessible," Tag quickly improvised.

Dixon narrowed his eyes. Hopefully he was thinking if Tag was stuck in the wheelchair, he couldn't snoop into any of the upstairs rooms. And Tag really hoped the kinkier goings-on in which Dixon was rumored to indulge happened in private.

Red didn't need to see that kind of stuff. For some reason, Tag wanted to protect her. Which was bizarre. Maybe because she was one of the few women who never came on to him. Almost any other woman put in the situation she'd been in over the past week would have been aggressive with him, sexually and financially. It was actually kind of nice to be the one pursuing her. But what would he do with her if he caught her? That was a problem.

They could never be anything other than friends. And right now, he was going to lend his friend a hand.

Red looked pale. Tag thought her chef whites might be leeching the color from her face, but from the way she flinched when Franz rolled him into the kitchen, he had to wonder if something else was going on.

"Tag." She wet her lips with her tongue, sending his mind places it shouldn't go. "What are you doing here?"

"I told you I was going to help you. Didn't you believe me?"

"How can you help from a wheelchair?" Her voice was squeaky.

"Please notice my costume." He was proud of what he'd done. Or rather, what Hans had accomplished despite being surly about it. "You put what you want served on my table. I roll around the party, offering hors d'oeuvres. Except the deviled eggs. I may eat those myself." He forced himself to grin, because

Red seemed distracted. "Hey. You'll be fine," he continued in a softer voice. "You worked damned hard. Dixon will be pleased."

The muscles in her exposed throat worked convulsively, almost as if she were gulping down water.

"What's wrong?" Tag asked.

"What?"

"I don't mumble, Red. You're as nervous as a..." He groped for a metaphor. "As a rookie his first time at bat, bottom of the ninth, bases loaded, tie game, two outs." Yeah, she was that nervous.

She focused on him. "I just have a lot on my mind."

She was lying. Her gaze sliding away from his, the sudden jerk of her head when someone at the party laughed too loudly, and the trembling in her fingers all gave her away. She shouldn't be as tense as she was. Feeding the baseball team was much more stressful than a millionaire's...

Unless Dixon had done something to make her so jittery.

"Do you want Franz to stay here with you?" Tag asked.

Red shook her head. "No. I'm fine. Really. And I appreciate you showing up to help." Her smile was forced, but he wasn't going to sit there and argue with her.

"So where's my first load of munchies?" he asked. Maybe if he could get her to concentrate on business, she'd relax a little.

She placed a tray with funny-looking round things on his table. Toothpicks with those colored ruffle things on one end were stuck into the tops of whatever it was.

"Mummy meatballs," she said.

Once she identified them, he could see where the pastry looked like strips of sheet and the sliced black olives as eyes.

The party rooms were dimly lit. Heavily scented candles flickered and filled the air with something that would probably give him a headache before too long. He thought he saw a head in a jar. He definitely saw a doll's head with an orange light glowing through the eyes and mouth holes. Creepy.

His was the worst costume in the place. Of course, a Dixon guest list wouldn't include the DIY set. Elaborate half-masks covered most of the faces, leaving only the wearers' mouths exposed.

"Mummy meatball?" he murmured as he approached one group of people.

"How cute." The woman's tone was condescending.

Tag wanted to cram the tray into her face. Man, he hated this sort of elitist thing. Everyone was so superior and snotty.

The meatballs went quickly. He checked on the buffet table before returning to the kitchen. The shrimp brains had been decimated. Most of the deviled eggs were gone. He hadn't seen all the variations on fingers Red had come up with, but he was impressed by what remained on the table. Especially the long green ones that turned out to be asparagus.

Franz rolled him back to the kitchen.

And so the routine continued for the next hour or so. Red seemed to relax and regain some of her sass and confidence. The food was a hit, even if Dixon's guests ignored the clever presentation Red had worked so hard on.

But as the evening wore on, the atmosphere of the party shifted. At first, Tag merely saw a few tongues being swapped. The half-masks were handy for that. When pieces of the elaborate costumes started slipping and revealing other bits, of course he looked. He was a heterosexual male and liked tits as much as the next red-blooded guy. And watching a woman on her knees in front of a man, her head bobbing, reminded him of some of things he wanted to share with Red. Again, the half-masks were a great idea.

And he'd figured there would be a sexual element to Dixon's party. According to the rumors he'd heard, *party* was code for *orgy*. Tag was glad Red's server called in sick. The poor girl might have been shocked. Or even worse, forced to participate. The same gossip hinting at sex fests also murmured about hush money. If Tag could keep Red in the kitchen, they might just get through the night and have their own good time later on back at his penthouse.

But why didn't these costumed creatures take their sexcapades upstairs?

The stink from the candles was starting to mingle with smells Tag usually didn't mind—semen and female arousal. The fucking had begun.

Tag rolled to the kitchen. Red was loading the dishwasher. "I don't think they're going to want any more food. Let's call it a night."

"I can't." Her smile was tired. Maybe even a little forced. "I have to clean up. That's where Gina comes in handy. No offense."

"None taken. But it could be a while. The festivities have begun."

Her coppery eyebrows tried to meet over her nose. "Festivities? Are you trying to tell me these guys are devil worshippers or whatever it is pagans do on Halloween?"

"If only," he muttered. "Franz, you think you can help me to the bathroom?"

SKYE KNEW SHE was being ridiculous for the relief she'd felt when Tag had shown up. He wasn't a hero except to the Gems. He wasn't her protector. He was her fuck buddy. But Drake Dixon was giving her a serious case of the creeps, and she somehow felt safer since Tag's arrival.

She told Franz where the facilities were. Once she was alone in the kitchen again, the sense of something being off returned. Maybe it was the devil worship that was not sitting well with her. The sooner she could leave Dixon's house, the happier she would be.

She decided to peek at the buffet table to get a better sense of what needed to be done. Maybe she could unobtrusively start clean up.

What she saw in that party room would never leave her.

Sex. Everywhere. Involving everyone. Very few people remained in costume, although most still wore their masks. The background music was eerie and deep, like bunches of men chanting. Naked bodies writhed, almost in rhythm to the sound. Even the flickering of the candles adopted the cadence. One knot of people turned out to be a woman and four men. Skye had heard about ménages and such, but the mechanics had never interested her. She was getting an education now.

Slowly, she started to back out of the room. Hopefully everyone was too engrossed in what they were doing to notice her.

Arms slid around her waist as she backed into a body. "Well, well."

She recognized that low voice, and it wasn't Tag or Franz. She arched her spine, but Dixon's grip was too tight.

"Ready to join the party?" His breath was hot against her ear.

"I'm on cleanup detail." She was amazed the words made it out of her throat. "But it can wait. I don't want to disturb your guests."

One of his hands slid up her ribs, found a breast, and squeezed, not gently either. "Oh, don't be a spoilsport, Skye."

"I'm not a sport at all. I'm a cook. The caterer." Oops. Maybe shouldn't have reminded him she was just the help. Maybe he was one of those throwbacks who thought the household help was there to be exploited.

Where was Tag? Maybe he was stuck in a wheelchair and couldn't physically fight Dixon, but surely he would help her.

"Really, Mr. Dixon." She struggled against his arms. "You need to let me go back to the kitchen and do my job."

"Your job is to do what I tell you. And I have wanted to fuck you since you applied for the job at the stadium."

Everything inside her stilled. No wonder she'd never been comfortable around Dixon. It wasn't just a boss-versus-worker thing. In a way, what he said was a form of stalking.

"You do like your job at the stadium, don't you? It's been a profitable season for you."

"Are you saying if I want my contract renewed, I have to have sex with you?"

He squeezed her breast again. Nudged her backside with his erection. "That could be an interpretation."

She was going to have to burn her whites.

TAG MOTIONED FOR Franz to stop pushing his chair. A very naked mask-wearing man was groping Red. Tag recognized the mask. Dixon. Red appeared to be struggling, and that really pissed off Tag. He pulled his phone from his pocket and started recording the scene. Then he handed the phone to Franz and gestured for him to keep recording.

His chair was silent as he rolled closer. The rubber wheels barely whispered against the carpet.

"Are you saying if I want my contract renewed, I have to have sex with you?" The quaver in Red's voice pierced him.

"That could be an interpretation."

Tag debated whether to interfere or let Dixon finish hanging himself.

"I can get other catering jobs. I don't like being threatened."

"Not in this town."

"That is sexual harassment. It's illegal."

Dixon's chuckle triggered another rush of rage in Tag. "It's your word against mine. And besides. You need a building to work from."

"I have a building."

"Not after tomorrow," Dixon said.

The truth finished leeching the color from Red's face. "You're the reason I can't get an extension on my loan. You're the one buying my mortgage."

"You know about that?" Dixon's low laugh drew goose bumps on Tag's arms. Time to butt in.

"That's an awful lot of trouble to go through for a piece of ass," Tag said as he rolled out of the shadows. "You should be flattered, Red. He's willing to pay a lot for you."

Dixon turned to face Tag, bringing Red around like a shield. "This isn't your business."

"Sure it is. Red's a good friend of mine." He might be in a wheelchair, but Dixon was naked. Tag figured they were about even. "She's such a good friend, I'm willing to take her mortgage off your hands."

"I repeat. Not your business."

"You might want to get your hand off her breast too. It's really annoying me. I'm pretty sure she doesn't like it either."

He didn't dare look at Red's face. He might be too tempted to try to throw a punch, which wasn't a real good idea considering his physical limitations. And he couldn't ram Dixon's shins with his wheelchair, because the man was hiding behind Red.

Dixon ran his tongue down the side of Red's neck. Tag thought she tried to bury an elbow in Dixon's lean gut, but he couldn't be sure. "Find your own cunt. I think Terra Baldwin is in the other room. Purple feathers and silver-beaded mask."

A muscle twitched in Tag's jaw as he clenched his teeth. Dixon was only trying to distract him. Besides, his relationship with Terra was between him and Terra. If lying to him about her whereabouts so she could fuck other people was what she wanted to do, who was he to stop her?

Unlike stopping Dixon. Because Red clearly did not want to get naked with him.

"Let her go."

"You forget yourself. Or at least forget who you're talking to. I can trade you to the worst team in the American League. I can trade you to Japan. So back off and mind your own business."

"I guess you didn't hear me. Or didn't hear Ms. Schuyler."

"Let go of me." Red's voice rang out clear and strong. "I have no interest in participating in your party. You signed my standard contract. You hired me to cater. Nothing else."

Dixon dropped his arms. "A misunderstanding."

Red scurried away from Dixon. Ended up behind the wheel-chair.

"My ass." Tag managed to keep his tone mild despite the churning in his gut. "I heard you threaten her."

Dixon shrugged.

Scrawny-shouldered bastard. Maybe his build and his small dick were why he indulged in orgies.

"Your word against mine."

"I witnessed your threat."

"You'd do well to think about Japan before you say anything else."

"And I witnessed that threat," Red said.

"Maybe you'd better leave. Both of you." Dixon started to return to his guests.

"Not until you agree to sell the mortgage on Skye's the Limit to me."

Red kicked the back of his chair. Temper, temper.

Dixon snorted. "You can't threaten me. And if I hear even a breath about what transpired here today, I assure you that you will regret it. And you, Ms. Schuyler. Perhaps you ought to read the codicil I added to your contract."

"Franz?" Tag called. "You still there?"

The night nurse stepped into view, holding Tag's phone.

"You get all that?"

"Yes. And it's still recording."

The hall was too dim to be certain, but Tag thought Dixon lost a couple of shades off his tan. A quick glance down confirmed his dick had shriveled.

"No cell phones allowed at my parties. Didn't you read the codicil?" Dixon lunged toward Franz.

Red stuck out her foot as Tag replied, "I didn't sign a contract with you."

Dixon tripped over Red's leg and went sprawling onto the carpet, giving Tag a much clearer look at his ass than Tag ever wanted to see.

"Yet," Tag continued. "The only contract I will sign for you is for the purchase of Ms. Schuyler's mortgage."

"I will destroy you," Dixon snarled. "You're done as a baseball player."

"And you're going to make sure the Gems hire Skye's the Limit for, I don't know, maybe five seasons. Red, that good with you?"

Her eyes were wide. Her lips were moist and parted. Tag felt his cock stir. "Sure."

"My agent will be in touch with you in the morning about the mortgage. And don't even think about trying to fuck with me, Dixon, unless you want an instant replay on the Internet. Come on, Red. We're out of here."

Skye's hands shook as she tried to insert her key into the ignition of her van. All her trays and her presentation pieces. Abandoned. But she couldn't stick around to retrieve them. Or go back. Ever.

"You okay?"

Franz stood outside the driver's door with Tag beside him.

Skye unrolled the window. "Did I forget to say thank you?" Her voice trembled, and her vision was blurry from wetness.

"You can thank me later. I'm going to e-mail the video to you and to my agent. You might want to send a copy to your lawyer."

People like her didn't have lawyers, but Tag didn't need to know that.

"Let's talk when we get back to my place."

"I'm going home," she said.

"No, you're coming back to my place. I don't trust Dixon, and you'll be safer with me and Franz than alone in an old building with a leaky gas stove."

Everything Tag said was true. Her hands started shaking even more. And Tag, so much lower than her, must have noticed.

"Are you all right to drive?"

"I'm okay."

"You're more than okay. But I don't want to have put my career on the line if you're going to wrap your van around a telephone pole."

She smiled. It felt crooked and scared, but it was real. "Okay. I'll follow you back to your place."

"Uh-uh. We're following you."

"Pour her something strong," Tag told Franz. He was still in his wheelchair although they were in his living room. "Like a brandy. And thanks for helping out."

"I don't want anything to drink." Red was huddled in the corner of the love seat. Her teeth chattered.

"Then get her a blanket," Tag snapped.

"I'm fine."

"You're in shock," Franz said. "I'm the health care professional here. I don't tell you how to soufflé a fish. You don't tell me how to treat shock."

"You don't soufflé a fish," she muttered.

"See what I mean?" Franz vanished down the hall.

"Let him do his thing," Tag said. "I pay him enough money."

"Okay." Her voice was small, as if she were disappearing inside herself.

"I hope you're not blaming yourself for what happened tonight." Tag didn't see any reason to avoid the conversation. Red was tougher than she thought she was.

"You tried to warn me. All I could think about was the money." There was a wet quality to her voice, as if she were swallowing tears.

Thank God. He couldn't deal with a weepy woman.

"I didn't know anything for sure," he said. "All I've ever heard are rumors."

"If you hadn't warned me in advance—"

"You still would have been okay. You're not a pushover."

"If you hadn't been there—"

"You'd have found some way to lodge his balls in his throat." He wasn't going to let her wallow in what-ifs. He was grateful he had been there. Grateful his instincts had warned him Dixon was up to no good.

"You know, when he kept showing up to supposedly check on the party, I didn't get a good feeling. He made me nervous."

"Showed up? Where?"

"At my place. A couple of times. I couldn't figure out how he knew where my building was. And he stopped me after the second game of the series." She shuddered. "He was always...touching my arm. My shoulder."

Franz returned with a blanket, which he draped over and around her, cocooning her like a mummy. "You know, I see a lot of things in my work," he said. "And I need to be discreet. Otherwise, I won't get hired to go into people's homes to help them. But in this instance, I can make an exception. If you two want to press charges or need another witness, I'll do it."

"Thank you," Red said.

"Probably won't be necessary, but if you want to swear out an affidavit for my agent to keep on file, I wouldn't fire you." Tag knew Dixon really could fuck with the rest of his career.

"That would work. I'll leave you two alone now. I'm sorry that had to happen to you, Skye. You're good people." And with that, Franz took himself off to wherever he kept himself until Tag called him.

"Why do you want to buy my mortgage?" Red asked after several moments of silence.

"Because you don't deserve to lose your building due to bad timing. I will give you a fifteen-day extension on your balloon payment. You've got game six of the Series tomorrow night."

"I can't let you—"

"I'm not paying off your mortgage, and I'm not buying your building. The only difference will be me holding the loan. The bank will still service it. You're still independent, building your business on your own. I said fifteen days, not fifteen weeks, not fifteen months, and not fifteen years. Days. Besides, there's no *letting*. I'm fucking with Dixon."

"Why?"

"I like you. I mostly like that you don't want anything from me. We're friends with benefits, and benefits aren't limited to sex." He shifted in his wheelchair and yawned. "Now roll me down to my room while I call Franz to get me ready for bed. Give me about half an hour. Then join me so I can show you some of the other benefits."

NOVEMBER 1, WORLD SERIES GAME 6

S kye swallowed a yawn and struggled to keep her eyes open as Tag's kitchen wavered around her. She hadn't slept at all, despite his best efforts to wear her out. Dawn meant hitting the produce market and then figuring out a menu for the returning Columbia Gems based on what she found there.

And of course she fretted about her serving pieces and the cleanup at Dixon's. Cleanup was part of her contract. Not only would she lose her best trays, platters, and such, but Dixon might not pay her.

She needed that money. She needed her equipment.

At least some of her frustration could be taken out on the chicken breasts. All she needed to do was pretend each slimy slab of poultry was Dixon's face—or other parts of his anatomy—as she savaged it with her meat mallet.

"Whack it a few times for me," Tag said.

Skye started. She hadn't heard him roll into the kitchen. "I don't know what you're talking about."

Tag snorted. "You're substituting the chicken for what you'd like to do to Dixon. What we'd both like to do to Dixon."

"Don't be ridiculous. I'm just worried about my serving pieces."

"I hired someone to clean up," Tag said. "And before you get all pissy about it, it's my fault you left the party early."

No, it wasn't. She wanted to cry, raise her face to the heavens, and howl. Instead, she reached for another chicken breast. "By rescuing me?" She could have been raped. If Tag hadn't...

"I didn't rescue you. You're the one who tripped him. I just guaranteed our getaway."

She brought her mallet down on the plastic-wrap-encased chicken. Smashed through it all the way to the marble counter.

"Man, are you going to have fun slicing all that zucchini." Tag nodded toward the pyramid of yellow and green summer squashes. "I think I'm going to leave you alone for a while."

Tag's mind was not on the physical therapy, and Bluto gave him shit for his lack of concentration.

Instead of focusing on reps and the pain Bluto was so fond of inflicting, Tag thought about hiring a bodyguard for Red when she went to the stadium that night. But procuring credentials to get someone during the regular season was a hassle, so postseason would be tougher. The best he could do was to go with her himself. Because Dixon was going to be there. How could the majority shareholder of the Gems not show up when the Gems could clinch the Series at home?

And Dixon knew Red would be there.

Tag swallowed the bitterness building in the back of his throat. He'd purposely stayed away from the stadium for games one and two. If he was going to be there, he should be wearing his chest protector, his leg guards, and his mask. He should be crouched behind home plate, not in a wheelchair.

And if he knew Red at all, he knew she wouldn't back down. She might be scared to death, but when it came to her job, she would be willing to risk facing Dixon less than twenty-four hours after his assault on her. Besides, there were plenty of out-of-way nooks in the bowels of the stadium. Tag wasn't familiar with Red's routine or how the luxury suites were serviced, but he did not want her alone and vulnerable.

Tag knew Dixon would be wary around him. The video was too damaging for him to ignore. Marty had a different view of the video: blackmail, he'd called it. He wanted Tag and Red to press charges.

"I'm not going to use this in your contract negotiations. I don't use extortion to conduct business."

Tag had to respect Marty's stance.

But that didn't help Red.

Skye kept her smile in place as she stood behind the serving station in the Gems' clubhouse. So far, the evening had gone pretty much close to normal except for the tension in the players. A minor commotion by the doors had her scanning the open space for Dixon. Maybe she was jumpier than usual, but after what had happened the previous evening, she wasn't surprised.

What did surprise her was when Tag rolled his way into the serving line. He'd been the source of the hubbub in the clubhouse.

"What are you doing here?" she asked. "I was going to come back to watch the game with you after I dropped the leftovers at the shelter."

"I just want to make sure you're not rooting for Seattle. That might upset the guys." He said it as if he was joking.

Adam Chrestler, who was next in line, punched Tag's bicep. "Don't pick on Skye. She might start serving slop like we had in Seattle." Skye thought about revising her negative opinion of Chrestler. Until he said, "I didn't know you two were a thing."

"We're not a thing," Skye said.

"The team hired her to cook for me," Tag said at the same time.

Chrestler snickered as he filled his plate with grilled chicken, summer squashes, and bell peppers. "I think I'm going to start a rumor about you guys."

"Darn," Skye snapped. "I forgot to bring your chocolate laxative dessert."

"You should start working on your fastball or your sinker." Tag's tone wasn't any warmer than hers. "You know, instead of hassling the help."

Chrestler snorted and moved on.

The help. Right.

Tag wouldn't be at the stadium without one of his hired hands. "Where's Franz?" she asked as she served the next player.

"In the car. We're not going to be here that long." Tag rolled his chair to her side of the table.

Skye hated to admit it, but she relaxed a bit once she knew Tag was at the stadium. She hadn't realized how tense she was until she saw him.

"Who's serving the boxes and suites?" Tag asked after the last player straggled through the food line.

"Food-service workers."

"That's good."

"That's standard."

He had nothing to add, so she started packaging the leftovers for the homeless shelter. He moved away from the tables, settling out of the light to watch. Her. Because the game wasn't due to start for another couple of hours.

Simply having him nearby reassured her.

When she was finished and ready to roll her coolers to her van, Tag said, "If we hurry, we can catch the first pitch at home."

Home. His penthouse. But she couldn't stay there forever. Once she'd taken delivery of her new stove, she could move back to the third floor of her building. Tag had already started the process of buying her mortgage.

A movement in the shadows snagged her attention. The rumble of the cooler wheels on the uneven pavement masked any sound. She couldn't be certain, but her gut said it might be Dixon.

She didn't want to spend the rest of her life flinching at random flickers in the corners of her eyes.

THAT WASN'T TOO bad.

Tag's first appearance at the ballpark since his injury wasn't as uncomfortable as he'd thought it would be, and that was good. It helped that he'd avoided areas where he might encounter the media. Most of the guys were too tightly wound about the upcoming game to give him much grief. Not that they would even be in the Series if it hadn't been for him.

"Baseball is the only place in life where a sacrifice is really appreciated." He'd heard that quote once and laughed. Wasn't so funny now. Did his teammates appreciate his sacrifice? No one had alluded to his injury except to say it was great to see him. No one had said, *Wish you were behind the plate tonight.*

"I'm really grateful you came to the stadium tonight," Red said as she hung her jacket in his hall closet. "I didn't realize how nervous I was until I got there."

"Another benefit of friendship," Tag muttered.

Her lush lips curved in a smile that shot straight to his groin.

"Let's watch the game. Then you can show me exactly how grateful you are."

Her smile morphed to a smirk. A teasing, flirty, bad-girl smirk. "Only if Seattle wins."

The Gems lost, three nothing.

NOVEMBER 2, WORLD SERIES GAME 7

Tag was grumpy all day. Skye wished she knew him well enough to ask how he felt about the game, but although they'd become friends since his injury, although he had rescued her from Drake Dixon, and although they were having amazing sex, she still didn't know who Tucker Alexander Gentry was. Still didn't understand what made him tick.

She only knew how to entertain him.

He'd eaten his early dinner of grilled salmon and steamed green beans—the same meal she was serving the team for their pregame spread—in silence.

Finally, she couldn't take any more.

"You don't need to come to the stadium with me if it bothers you." She was taking a stab in the dark, but he'd been broody since the game six loss.

"I don't trust Dixon."

Handy excuse.

"He won't try anything in public," she said. Not that she was convinced she was safe. Her illusion of invulnerability had been shattered.

"It would be too easy for him to get you alone."

"He won't. I'm putting my faith in your phone insurance." She had to. She inhaled deeply. "So if going to the stadium makes you feel weird or anything, you really don't need to play guardian angel to me. Not that I don't appreciate it. But—"

"Why would I feel weird?" Tag snapped. He glared at her, not blinking. Not moving at all except for the rise and fall of his chest as he breathed. "I don't feel anything except wanting my team to win. Something you should think about. What was it you said to me? Don't bite the hand that feeds you?"

"I 'm cheering for the Gems tonight."

"It's about time. You should have been rooting for them all along."

Tag knew why she'd wanted Seattle to win. To bring it up again now told her he was trying to deflect her attention away from him by putting her on the defense.

"You're absolutely right. I am scum."

She was going to miss Tag. Even when he was surly. Oh, she still might see him every day when she cooked his meals, but once she had her new stove in place, she'd only be dropping off the food.

She knew her only value was in keeping him entertained.

The final game of the season. The Gems had pushed the Series to game seven. The clubhouse almost hummed with the players' energy. Their entire season had come down to this November evening.

The pregame meal was uneventful. Cleaning went smoothly. Skye and Tag were settled in front of his television by the bottom of the first inning.

"What do you think of the wings?" Skye asked as Tag gnawed on a bone in the commercial break between the top and bottom of the second. She'd prepared two kinds for him to snack on during the game: one with bourbon sauce and a beer-battered version.

"Not bad."

"I'm experimenting with healthier versions for my election night job. I'm probably going to need to keep using your kitchen until I can get my new stove." There. She'd put it out there for him to accept or reject.

"No problem. Are these left wings or right wings?"

Skye laughed. She was going to miss the camaraderie of watching games with him. His wry humor.

"What else are you serving?" he asked.

"Pulled pork sliders."

He snorted. "Kool-Aid?"

"I hadn't thought of that. It's not a bad idea. I thought caramelized acorn squash rings and—"

"Suckers for dessert."

"I beg your pardon?" What was he talking about?

"Lollypops. We called 'em suckers when I was a kid. Appropriate for politicians and their supporters, don't you think?"

Yeah, she was going to miss hanging out with him.

RED WOULDN'T BE in his place cooking every day.

Tag couldn't wrap his head around the idea. She'd become a necessity in his life over the past two weeks. He'd miss her more than he'd miss Bluto, Hans, or Franz when they finished with him.

The only thing going right with him was how quickly the bank was handling his purchase of Red's mortgage after Dixon backed off. And maybe the Gems winning the World Series.

He settled in his recliner and tried to focus on the game, but Red had distracted him with the reminder of her temporary status.

During the commercials between the third and fourth innings, he reopened the subject. "How long before you can get a stove?"

"Trying to get rid of me?"

The teasing tone didn't help his mood.

"Just trying to get a handle on things."

"Thanks to you, I can make my balloon payment as soon as my check from the Gems clears."

If Dixon didn't delay her payment.

"Once that's behind me, I can take out a loan to buy the stove of my dreams."

"A loan to buy a stove?"

"The stove I want costs over eight thousand dollars."

He turned from the TV to look at her. "That's ridiculous. What is it? Gold-plated or something?"

"You paid more for your car, and the stove will last longer and pay for itself. Your car depreciated the moment you drove it off the lot."

The game resumed. The score remained nothing to nothing.

Tag should have been thinking about how Win Winston ought to pitch to the Seattle line-up. Instead, he conjured scenarios that would get Red to stay with him. Only until he was on both feet again. Nothing long-term.

"So tell me what's going on with the pitches," Red asked.

That was one to keep his mind from picturing her naked, her long red curls tickling his thighs while her tongue tickled…

"Wes is calling for a changeup away." He wondered how he could convince Red to sit on his lap. If there were any way he could join her on the sofa, he would have. Stupid broken leg.

"How do you know that?"

"He's waggling four fingers. Then three taps to his thigh."

There was the thigh thing again. Tag would like to waggle something against one of Red's thighs.

"I don't get it."

Oh, he'd love to give it to her. Again. And before the game was over.

"Four fingers is a changeup and an odd number of taps means away. When Wes touched his mask, he indicated to Win that the second set of signals was the pitch. All the other stuff is just to confuse the runner on second." Wait. When had Seattle gotten a runner on base? "Now stop talking and pay attention to the game."

"I am paying attention to the game. That's why I'm asking questions."

He liked that she didn't back down. What he didn't like was the way she'd gotten to know him too well so quickly. Terra never would have picked up on his reluctance to go to the stadium. Too subtle for the woman chasing the extreme story. For the woman Dixon claimed was fucking her brains out at his Halloween orgy when she'd told Tag she was out of the country.

And he still couldn't summon the energy to waste on being upset either at Terra for lying—if she had—or at Dixon for thinking his relationship with Terra was a weak spot. Especially when he compared his reaction about Terra to what he'd seen Dixon do to Red.

Two batters later, Seattle scored a run.

The score didn't change. The Gems stranded two runners in the bottom of the seventh inning, but going into the bottom of the ninth, the score was one-nothing, Seattle.

"Hey, Red. How about a kiss for luck?"

She hauled herself off the sofa and sauntered toward him, hips swaying so provocatively, his half-hard cock stirred. The odd thing was she wasn't trying to seduce him. She probably had no idea just how much she turned him on.

He wrapped his fingers around her slender wrist as she leaned in to kiss him. One gentle tug and she was on his lap.

"That's better," he said. And it was.

Until she started squirming against him. Not to get away, but to make herself more comfortable. He pressed his cock against her soft ass.

A wild pitch hit Wes in the arm. He walked to first.

Tag nipped Red's neck while Seattle's pitcher shook off his catcher. The Gems' backup closer was at the plate. One of the reasons he was the backup closer was because he could hit as well as pitch his way out of a jam. Seattle had been burned by him in game four.

Red arched away from Tag's mouth. "Pay attention to the game," she said as she reached between them and cupped his balls.

Right.

The first pitch was high and inside. As was the second. The closer swung at the third for his first strike. And all the while, Red was fondling Tag's erection.

"I'll get you for this," he said.

"I'm planning on it," she replied.

The crack of maple wood against cowhide, a sound Tag alternately loved and hated, stilled Red's hand and stilled his labored breathing.

The white ball soared against the black night sky. Flew past the infield. Past the outfield. Past the first tier of seats in left field.

Two-run home run. Holy shit.

"Holy shit!"

The Columbia Gems won their first-ever World Series.

I hope you enjoyed CATCHER INTERFERENCE, the first of three novellas featuring Tag and Skye.

If you'd like to stay up to date with my news and exclusive content, please subscribe to my newsletter

Also By

SHIFTER ROMANCE

TOKE LOBO & THE PACK SERIES

Moonlight Serenade

And Jericho Burned

Omega Moon Rising

SERVICE FOR SANCTUARY SERIES

Betrayed by the Moon

Beware of the Moon

Besieged by the Moon.

STANDALONE MASH-UP NOVELLA

Shifting Home

STEAMY CONTEMPORARY ROMANCE WITH A HINT OF DANGER

COLUMBIA GEMS BASEBALL ROMANCES

Missing the Signs

Hit by His Pitch

Novella: Catcher Interference (Tag & Skye Book 1)

Novella: No Doubles Defense (Tag & Sky Book 2)

Novella: Batting Cleanup (Tag & Skye Book 3)

THE WRITE PLACE RETREAT ROMANCES

(Coming soon)

ABOUT THE AUTHOR

MJ Compton grew up near Cardiff, New York, a place best known for its giant—a hoax so successful, P.T. Barnum duplicated it. The tale of the "petrified man" convinced MJ that inventing stories could be a career.

Although her 30 years working in local television included such highlights as being bitten by a lion, preempting a US President for a college basketball game, giving a three-time world champion boxer a few black eyes, and meeting her husband, MJ never lost her dream of creating her own stories.

MJ still lives in upstate New York with her husband. Music and cooking are two of her passions, and she enjoys baseball, college basketball, and sitting on her patio on summer nights to count lightning bugs, but she's primarily focused on writing.